T0208816

WHEN
Women
BECOME
INVISIBLE

VICTORIA JANOSEVIC

WHEN WOMEN BECOME INVISIBLE

iUniverse books may be ordered through booksellers or by contacting:

iUniverse
1663 Liberty Drive
Bloomington, IN 47403
www.iuniverse.com
1-800-Authors (1-800-288-4677)

Because of the dynamic nature of the Internet, any web addresses or links contained in this book may have changed since publication and may no longer be valid. The views expressed in this work are solely those of the author and do not necessarily reflect the views of the publisher, and the publisher hereby disclaims any responsibility for them.

Any people depicted in stock imagery provided by Thinkstock are models, and such images are being used for illustrative purposes only. Certain stock imagery © Thinkstock.

ISBN: 978-1-5320-1849-7 (sc)
ISBN: 978-1-5320-1850-3 (e)

Library of Congress Control Number: 2017904856

Print information available on the last page.

iUniverse rev. date: 03/24/2017

Contents

Introduction

I chose the title *When Women Become Invisible* for my memoir because it aptly describes the real-life experience of many women at some point after they enter middle age. I know I'm not the only woman who's discovered the subtle changes that daily life introduces as age forty progresses to fifty and the not-so-subtle changes that take place later on. It's the experience of being overlooked and unnoticed to the point of eventually feeling invisible.

It first happened to me in a Home Depot parking lot. I had to return a heavy bag of cement that my contractor hadn't used. I was in my early fifties then, and that day I'd worn no makeup and was in plain and simple attire to run this humdrum errand. Realizing the bag was too heavy for me to lift out of the car trunk, I looked around for help. A young thirty something man was passing by.

"Excuse me," I said politely, "can you help me lift this bag from my trunk?"

"Bad back—sorry," he answered briskly, not breaking his stride for a moment as he turned to look my way. He was walking at a fast, easy clip, and I certainly couldn't detect any signs of back pain.

Meanwhile, a woman near my age saw the incident and then gazed at me meaningfully. "That was not very nice of him," she said. "Here. Let me help you."

Together we managed to haul the cumbersome sack into a shopping cart. Without speaking another word, we both knew why he had manufactured his feeble excuse.

The Home Depot incident marked the first time I knew things were not going to be the same anymore. It taught me what it feels like to be overlooked rather than looked at.

Living as we do in a youth-worshiping culture, not only in America but just about worldwide, women often discover that beauty and perfection feel required more than ever. Women of the proverbial certain age (usually somewhere past the age of forty) find that they have been granted a swift and compulsory divorce from mainstream popular culture and from relevance. This divorce decree is a rude, intangible document that verifies that they are not needed anymore, that they no longer reside in a hot, desirable demographic.

"What?" some women may protest. "I didn't file for divorce from relevance. I'm attractive, smart, and talented, and I still have much to contribute. Who decides that I don't count anymore?"

It's disconcerting and insulting for many women to watch their individual value on the sexual-desirability scale decrease and then vanish. We grow older, and one day—it happens. We notice life is different. We're overlooked. We're dismissed. We're ignored.

And we notice that no one is noticing us.

I was passionately driven to write this book. Why? First, because it was written as I traversed this new era in my life. The pages that follow will tell you about some of my personal highs and lows regarding aging, beauty, and desirability and how I've managed to handle them. Second, I wrote it also for other women who can relate to some of my experiences and who, I hope, can benefit from what I'm sharing. I want to remind women of a certain age that you are not alone. Most of all, I realize that as I've learned and grown and encouraged myself, I can be a positive voice of encouragement and renewed joy to others along the way.

Society can be quite superficial. We place so much value on the physical; it clouds a judgment of the real value of a person. The Bible has ten commandments, and these days it seems society has added an eleventh unspoken one: "You shall not age!"

I hope that in reading this you can move past this unspoken commandment and embrace the inevitable aging as a new phase of life to enjoy. You can look forward to more positive things, to being yourself, to no longer worrying (it is the most unproductive of all human activities), and to facing each problem as it comes your way with grace and inner beauty.

If there's one thing I want you to take away from this book, it's this: you're not invisible; you're invincible!

Chapter 1

THE PRINT LOOKED
A LITTLE BLURRY

IT HAPPENED DURING my early forties. I was scrutinizing the movie listings in a local newspaper sometime in 1992 to find show-times for a movie. But there was a mysterious film over all the print, like a gauzy film. The truth is I had been through this gauzy-film experience when reading for some time, making most anything in print look a little blurry. Thinking there might be some kind of irritation in my eyes, I rubbed them whenever this happened. And rubbed them. And rubbed them.

Rubbing didn't help.

My friend Richard was with me that day. He was a close friend who also happened to be a physician.

I shook the newspaper in frustration. "You know, Richard, lately I've been having problems when I read. I'm just not seeing clearly. It must be something in my eyes—an irritation maybe? What do you think?"

"There's nothing in your eyes, Victoria," he replied without hesitation. "Your vision is at a different stage now. Your eyes are not focusing as sharply anymore. It sounds like you just need reading glasses."

"What? Are you sure?" Reading glasses? Weren't they just for old ladies? I didn't want to believe him.

"Oh yes, I'm absolutely sure," he said with a small chuckle. "It happens to almost everyone at some point after forty."

I felt like it was the beginning of the end. From that moment on, I grew more and more critical of myself. That first gray hair, a dreaded line on my face—worse—a wrinkle! Then another and another, and before long, the mirror became my enemy.

Looking back now, twenty-five years later, I realize I was much too hard on myself. Still, with every glance in the mirror, I was seeing an ever-more alien version of myself, someone older. Even though I was lucky enough, not having gained any weight or showed as many gray hairs as some of my friends my age. I was still five foot three, still about 110 pounds, still had blonde hair and blue eyes. I'd even been compared to a younger Brigitte Bardot.

But this new woman in the mirror—an older woman—was me, like it or not. Yet my feelings, desires, and interests were the same as always. It was like the emergence of two separate lives. One of me was still thinking freely the way I think, unfettered by age, thinking of myself as young, energetic, and, of course, just as interesting as I had always been. But the second me began thinking of myself as older to reflect the ongoing changing image in the mirror.

My aging nagged me. It kept reminding me that time wasn't standing still for me. I scurried to conduct an informal survey of my friends, some of them my age and others somewhat older. They clued me in on things to come, on what to expect in the near future, and they were pretty negative about it all too.

"Oh, you'll feel your body becoming less agile.

As time goes by, you won't be able to do any heavy work like you used to."

"Then there are the aches and pains …"

"Your muscles get weaker and weaker."

"You'll be making more and more unwelcome trips to the doctor."

"It's awful! As if parts of your body are turning on you, little by little until they give in."

Not exactly a positive support group! Their collection of dreary forecasts brought to mind something Cher had said more than twenty years ago: "There's nothing good about turning fifty."

But true enough, my friends' negativity rang a distant alarm somewhere within me. Which of my two lives would take over? It is, after all, human nature to seek acceptance, approval, and social interaction. Based on my experience, I think that women are judged by their age and skin-deep appearance, and this makes for a genuine hardship in our aging progress. Who can deny it? True, some take it in stride, and I was curious to know how they do that. But why must my value as a person be based on how I look?

The older I got, the more I began to work on myself to upgrade a youthful appearance. I made sure I drank a lot of water, as I knew water was essential to the body. I used plenty of moisturizer cream. I made an effort to be as positive as possible. I also joined a health club and began dressing more youthfully. I knew these things were important to appear happy, or so I thought.

Who likes to get old anyway? I wondered. And no one is spared—rich, poor, plain, or beautiful. Favorable male attention—the looks, the whistles, the flirting and recognition I'd taken for granted (even enjoyed, I admit) for many years—was becoming extinct. So these were the first alerts that age was creeping up on me. My youthful looks were fading.

Piecing together each small experience, I realized this is another kind of body clock for women. Everyone is familiar with a thirty something woman's concern about her biological clock if, in fact, she wants to have children. But now, here was a different clock, a sex appeal clock ticking away like a scratched old record in my mind: *I don't have what it takes anymore to attract that kind of desire in a man. I don't have what it takes anymore.* Tick, tick, tick. Male reaction— or, perhaps more accurately, the absence of male reaction—was convincing. Tick, tick, tick. It wasn't my imagination. My sex appeal clock was ticking.

I don't want to sound boastful, but I was born with my fair share of what pop culture labels genetic blessings. I was petite and had long blonde hair and bright blue eyes. In my youth, I'd taken for granted my physical attractiveness. I never had a problem meeting a man whenever my friends and I went out for a drink. But here I was being robbed of my confidence. My sense of self-worth was evaporating. And having fun? Yet another option I was losing my grasp on, as I began to believe life couldn't be enjoyed anymore with the loss of sex appeal.

Sliding down to a bad place, I let myself grow disconnected from the world, allowing life to slowly pass me by. Disconnection. Irrelevance. If you want to feel irrelevant and disconnected from the world, this would be the place. And if I was persuaded that I deserved to feel lonely, this was that very bad place too. Two separate lives. One was my soul, my spirit thinking well of myself, free and easy. The second was the reality of my body, the aging woman in the mirror. The two lives could not coexist.

My personal fighting match against aging was on the horizon. Time to put on my boxing gloves.

Chapter 2

ENCOUNTERING INVISIBILITY

THAT INCIDENT IN the Home Depot parking lot had a lot of impact on me. The incident, however minor, got me thinking …

That evening, I took a quiet moment to collect my thoughts. Sitting on the couch, drink in hand, my mind drifted back to a time in my life when I was much more active. I'd been so full of energy and always on the go—doing volunteer work, riding my bicycle as much as possible to do either food shopping or visiting stores near me. I had a job in downtown Manhattan, and I eventually changed to a job closer to my house because the commute was a one-hour-plus train ride one way. That turned into two hours plus total for the day. It was just too much for me each day …

Was I really going in that direction? Losing interest in all the activity I used to enjoy so much? Was I ready? Looking at it this way, is anybody ever ready? One thing was certain. The Home Depot incident marked the first time I knew that my life was not going to be the same anymore.

The next morning, I did not wake up refreshed, energized, or with a new outlook. I felt no different than the night before, and what that felt like was depression, a person in mourning. I hoped it would pass. The truth is *that I was in mourning—for the years I lost and would never get back.* Many more nights followed like this. Waking up in the middle of the night, enclosed in a wretched blanket of silence and darkness, my insides were screaming, "I hate this!"

Everything began to look gray. And all I knew was that I wanted back the color of life.

However, compared to a twenty-year-old woman, for whom most any age group of men are available, many women after age forty and fifty feel that they're reduced to men who are the same age or older. This has started to change in the past twenty years, of course, but many women over age fifty were taught to look for a man who is not only older but richer, better educated, and taller. These are tough shoes to fill these days! Not only is that tough criteria to meet when you're in your twenties or thirties, but once you're in your forties or fifties, it's so much harder. The reality of sheer demographics shrinks our partner pool. Whether a woman marries or not, statistically, she is more likely to spend more of her retirement years alone than partnered due to the mortality rates of men. The unfortunate truth is they die younger than we do.

But I've also found that with this generation of men, someone over age fifty is at a mature age where sometimes the youthful temperament of expression is replaced by an insecurity of losing their macho image. Some fear that being with a mature woman would get them labeled as not macho. But I think that some of us contribute to this belief by not putting the effort into ourselves as we did when we where younger. We used to spend more times on our looks, and once past menopause, some of us seem to let go much of this by not making enough effort to look our best. From my own experience, I have noticed the difference in men when women do this.

If women are convinced that when we reach the age of menopause, we automatically lose our sex appeal to men, how good do we have to look to leave the lights on in our bedrooms during a moment of passion? How can a woman feel upbeat about herself, especially when the tabloids are constantly writing about how some actor in Hollywood has replaced an older partner with a much younger one? We see it almost every day on the front page of magazines like *Glamour*, *Cosmopolitan*, *People*, the *Enquirer*. All are magazines we find at the checkout register in many stores. Perhaps out of boredom while we wait for our turn, we might pick them up, and to pass the time, we read them.

Even if you don't read these types of magazines, you've probably observed this phenomenon in real life. Maybe your best friend's husband "traded her in" for a younger woman, leaving her shell-shocked—and poorer. Perhaps some of your coworkers have done the same thing or have been victimized by this trend. Maybe a neighbor had to move away after her husband downsized her life and up-sized his own.

A lot of the middle-age women also start

dressing down instead of dressing up. We become thrifty with ourselves, much too thrifty, and therefore lose that sex appeal. High-heel shoes are replaced by a flat slipper; the makeup we used to wear becomes nude and barely noticeable; our cleavage, legs, and buttocks are eliminated. But do we really have to dress like a twenty-year-old again with hot red lipstick, high heals, or big cleavage to get back that sex appeal we long for so much? And if we do get a look, every so often, maybe we don't acknowledge it with a smile out of the fear that it may not be sincere.

Therefore we become victims of a self-fulfilling prophecy, a self-fulfilled prediction. We are convinced that we are not being noticed. But we seem to forget that we brought this on ourselves by our questionable behavior, putting less effort into looking our best, which leaves no room to think otherwise. We have to learn to shut off this way of thinking. According to one study I read about in the German magazine *Die Neue Frau* (*The New Woman*), half of women believe that there is nothing positive to replace that lack of physical sex appeal we feel as we get older.

This is certainly not true! To be young, sure

it's beautiful, and men more likely will be coming up to you to offer you their help if needed. A survey in Germany was once taken where students who wanted to make extra money were hired to talk to men in public. They asked questions like what they like most in a woman, and to the researchers' surprise, men's top priority wasn't, in fact, to have a woman with those perfect breasts or immaculate legs. Behavioral researchers found out that attractiveness and youthfulness were actually number three on their list, right after credibility and reliability.

We should stop self-criticism and start listening to what others have to say, getting over that constant fear that we physically just can't hold a candle against youthfulness anymore. Thoughts like this are certainly no good for your self-confidence and sooner or later will negatively influence how men perceive you.

However, in reverse, we can change the outlook on how men see us by openness and sympathy, and we will automatically be looked at as being more attractive. Your inner radiance and outlook on life will shine more than a face without wrinkles. We don't need to hide in this respect. A woman after age forty can still have that radiance of charm, charisma, life experience, and self-assurance. With values like these, we will automatically have inner peace if we know that we don't need to constantly be in competition to prove ourselves to the opposite sex. In the end, we will be the ones whistling and holding our heads up high with pride and self-confidence.

From 1946 to 1964, we had the largest population growth in American history: the baby boomers. I was born between 1946 and 1964, and I know many of you reading this are in this same age group.

If you're feeling old and invisible, then I hope this book can offer some guidance.

Despite reading the surveys, and based on observations I made, I still had to convince myself that growing older and feeling invisible can have its positive points. The next chapter will show you more about those positives.

Chapter 3

HOLLYWOOD CALLING

THE DOUBLE STANDARD. What's a woman to do? Popular culture embraces it. Actually, pop culture is having a love affair with it.

It is the ageless double standard that has traditionally been an oppressor of girls and women in the sexual arena. But once it comes to passing the age of forty or fifty, the double standard is the inescapable status quo for women. Men are allowed to age, to grow older, and still be regarded as desirable and sexy. What men of a certain age want and what they think still matters.

Women, on the other hand, start losing currency fast when they enter the ranks of a certain age. So what else is new? Still, who could have predicted that in the twenty-first century, it's not getting better—it's getting worse. Just look at the messages we're pounded with from Hollywood, which serves as both a symbolic and literal example. We see leading men, actors in their fifties and sixties, who are paired with leading ladies who are young enough to be their daughters, sometimes their granddaughters! Think Michael Douglas and Gwyneth Paltrow in *The Perfect Murder*. Harrison Ford and Sean Connery, both septuagenarians, are still leading men, at least for as long as they want to be. Not so for actresses. Second leads and character roles await them, and sometimes only for the A-listers at that. Usually. Of course there are always exceptions here and there.

When I began my personal war with this opponent—aging—it was in the early 1990s. I was still a youngish-looking mid fortysomething. I felt many times that my mind and attitude did not go well with my physical changes, and from early on, I knew I would do whatever it took. So I resolved to fight, and to fight by any means necessary. Every time I looked in the mirror, it felt like I was looking at another wrinkle or gray hair. That meant yes, that cosmetic surgery or some kind of professional cosmetic assistance was looming in my future. And why not?

This culture always hears Hollywood calling, and the call says you are not allowed to age. Watching talk shows like *The Real* and *The View,* where the hosts and guests are groomed and dressed to perfection with perfect makeup, tailored designer clothes, and expensive accessories, is enough to make anyone feel less desirable. It can offer us the message that this is what a woman should look no matter what age. Why?

Because youth is king. Popular culture, as sustained by Hollywood, the fashion, music, and television industries, and Internet everywhere, says so. It often feels like there is no escape. Youth rules. And if youth is king, then beauty is its queen. However, I have also learned to ignore the pressure of the constant reminder, not listening to what is said on TV or written in magazines, as it only would fuel the flame.

Even if there is no TV in the house, we are still exposed to what is going on in the outside world. All we have to do is wait in line at any grocery store and see all the different magazines with huge headlines about the beauty of some famous person and how good they look in spite of age. To ignore this kind of advertising is not always easy; after all, you are reminded every single time you are waiting in line. An ordinary person dressed in a sweat suit with no makeup is never seen on the cover of any of these magazines. What is this telling us?

In the frenetic pursuit to be beautiful, females are taught a perverse, false truth: that their main value as a person is based on their youth, beauty, and sexuality. I'm not against youth, beauty, or being sexy, of course. Unfortunately, women have always been judged by the superficial standards of appearance and age.

Now there is an ever-increasing demand for the display of female sexual availability. Let your boobs hang out! This is the so-called side boobs exposure. Advertise your skin. Cleavage at the office, on the job, at the gym, in the grocery store, wherever. Subtlety? Forget it. Not anymore.

When I recall the American feminist movement that started in the 1970s, it was such a consciousness-raising force about women's roles. It certainly made me more aware of how badly we needed change—change in how women were perceived and what opportunities were available to them.

Here are a few facts to remind you of our progress: Before the changes in laws that were made in the 1970s, a woman could not sue her employer for sexual harassment, a woman wasn't paid the same as her male counterpart, a woman could not keep a job while pregnant, a woman could not have a credit card under her name, women were not allowed to fight in the military, a women could not refuse sex with her spouse, and there was no birth control if married. Women could not serve on a jury. So a lot of positive change has taken place of course.

But we are now living in a post-feminist world in which female-related social regression is alarming—to me, anyway. I'm hoping that you, the reader, are identifying and agreeing with me, at least more often than not. As I see it, that battle to tone down and diminish superficial judgments and expectations of women has been lost. Do you remember the feminist outrage back in the seventies when the Rolling Stones album *Black and Blue* was released? There was outrage at the cover art that depicted a woman obviously battered and physically bruised. Can you imagine such a response now? Would anyone notice? I wonder.

In the end, if it makes money, well, it's just a fashion statement, or radical chic, or some postmodern logic. The pop stars are unabashedly slutty looking. Think Miley Cyrus and Nicki Minaj. Even Taylor Swift has sexed up her all-American-girl image. And stars who push back against the status quo, like Nikki Traynor, are still criticized for their looks.

And so, regrettably, I say that battle has been lost. I honestly believe we will not be seeing a reversal in pop culture's demands on young women and girls to display themselves. It doesn't even matter that it's not really sexy. If you want male approval and attention, give them what they want. And what they want is skin and that hint of sexual availability.

A thirty something friend of mine named Angi still gets indignant at flagrantly sexist advertising of a popular women's clothing mogul (not to be identified here!). I've tried explaining to her that it's too late. The battle was already lost. Exhibiting the naked or near-naked female body has become more accepted than ever before, accepted as sexy and desirable and perfectly okay. Youthful skin being exposed in ways that keep pushing the envelope is here to stay. What it is teaching girls about their personal worth is ill fated and dangerous, I think. It leads them to believe that it's acceptable—even required—to dress in a way that shows a lot of skin, and it suggests that wearing as much makeup as possible is needed and expected in order to attract men.

To be young in the twenty-first century is maybe not so much to be envied. This excessive pressure on girls to be sexy and beautiful, pressure that was previously reserved for their later teenage and early adult years, has now invaded their childhood years. It does not need much of an explanation; all we need to do is look around. Children do not look like children anymore but rather like little adults Girls are starting to wear makeup younger and younger, accompanied by shorter skirts and tighter tops. There are reality televisions shows about beauty contests for children, some as young as toddlers!

Talking with friends close to me in age, all of

them baby boomers, there's a consensus among us about this terrible trend.

On my way out one day, I ran into my older neighbor Rose, who is about ten years my senior and someone I talk with about the changes in life.

"Oh, hello, Vicky," she said cheerfully. "How are you doing and how is life treating you?"

"I am doing fine, Rose, other than keeping my mind off the subject."

"What subject are you talking about?"

"The changes in life and what comes with it."

She sighed, looking exasperated. "Are you telling me you are still on it?"

"Yes," I admitted. "You know, it's not something that can be switched off like a switch."

"Vicky, look at me!" she said sternly. "I'm about ten years your senior, and yes, I admit I am not excluded from feeling and thinking like this, but at one point I also realized it's something I cannot change! I'm not saying that it does not cross my mind every so often, but I also know I cannot have these thoughts take over and control my life."

"I guess you're right. After all, you had more than ten years' experience to have thoughts of how to handle it. Believe me, I've gotten so much better already in dealing with these changes, but I still haven't been able to totally erase it out of my mind. I look around and often see young beautiful women and tell myself, 'I used to look that young.' It's not that easy to just not think otherwise."

"Give it time, Vicky," Rose answered. And she was right.

We all seem to feel and think the same when it comes to the subject of youth and especially of young women. The superficial perception of women being dismissed from relevancy based on these appraisals is getting worse. With the outward signs of aging—noticing changes in our skin, hair, and physical agility—we start to experience life differently.

During my forties, I began to see the world with different eyes, and not just ones augmented by my new reading glasses! Like from the outside looking into a universe that was different, I was seeing the favor that accompanies youth. Once I had a visitor from Germany staying at my house, and as he had no car, I loaned him a bicycle to get around. One day he got into a small accident;

he got hit by a car that was being driven by a very young girl. It was clearly the girl's fault. However, when we went to the police station to make a report, it was very noticeable that the police officer was leaning toward the young girl's story, even though he knew that the girl was in the wrong. He tried to change the story so it would look like it was no one's fault.

I was no longer a participant in the youth culture. And yet I had never noticed this reality before. It never dawned on me before how different life is when you're young and how neglected mature women might be feeling until I began to see for myself. It can be so lonely.

That study I read about in *Die Neue Frau,* a magazine published in Germany that caters to women and aging, also described what to expect when coming into menopause. It mentioned menopausal women who are convinced that there is nothing positive to replace their feeling of loss of physical attractiveness and sex appeal, which made me wonder. Was I one of them? Yes. I was not looking forward to menopause, and so I resolved to combat it, to fight back even if it meant cosmetic surgery or injections or facial fillers or even a face-lift. I was willing to do whatever might work for me. After all, Hollywood was calling.

So how good do we have to look anyway? How can my contemporaries and I feel good about ourselves while television, movies, tabloids, the Internet, and celebrity culture are constantly confirming that yes, menopausal women are sex-appeal-free? You don't need to be knowledgeable about what is said on TV, the Internet, in movies or magazines. I have not met anyone yet where sooner or later the subject of aging did not come up: overlooked, not sought after, not in demand, not a preferred demographic for advertisers. Invisible.

There are still frequent news flashes about the latest celebrity divorces and breakups in which the male partner invariably trades in his wife for a younger woman. Some friends of mine were divorced for that very reason. You don't have to be famous. It is hurtful and does have the power to steal self-esteem.

Maybe that's why one of the countless celebrity-gossip TV shows reported that even the most beautiful women in the public eye do not necessarily wake up in the morning looking perfect. I confess to watching a segment of a particularly cheesy program that showed before and after photos of certain young female celebrities. And I have to admit I was surprised. A lot of time and work goes into the creation of such perfection for the magazine spreads and movies we see. Images can be deceptive.

And of course Photo shopping, the digital revision of pictures, is now the norm. The real woman is smoothed out, lengthened out, whittled down, and airbrushed to perfection. How often we see photos of celebs of all ages before and after; it's like telling us no matter what age or how negatively or positively we were blessed by nature, this is what we could or should look like. So is it true that the beautiful celebs are happier about themselves than the non-famous, everyday women in America? I groaned when I picked up a magazine article headlined: "Does Being Beautiful Automatically Mean Being Happy?" Hmm, about as convincing as "Money isn't everything." But hey, we still need it, yes? While reading the article, I tried to put myself in their shoes, to imagine the pressure of fame, constantly being in the spotlight and being expected to look great all the time.

What did strike me was thinking about the scrutiny that this level of fame brings. For example, just think of one mistake in your own life that you made—something that was embarrassing, that you truly regretted. It doesn't even have to be that important. Then imagine having photographers and microphones shoved in your face about it and being the subject of unmerciful public criticism all while dealing with whatever your mistake may have been. And blow back on the Internet! Kind of unnerving, do you agree? How much more devastating aging can potentially be for a woman in the public eye.

I may have a unique perspective on this cultural pressure because I grew up in quite a different country with markedly different attitudes. I had a confining and abusive childhood in post–World War II Germany. My mother had been widowed twice before she met my father after the war, who was a prisoner of Germany. Although my parents lived together for a few years, both of them worked during the day. My mother was a teacher, and my father a translator of five languages. My mother was not what we call today a stay-at-home mom.

From her first marriage, she had two children, my older half brother and sister, both in there teens by the time I came along. Because she worked, she left me and my younger sister, Kristina, in our older sister's care during the day, which did not go over well with the neighbors. Complaints from these neighbors about the situation eventually reached the local authorities, and soon the government stepped in. Through government intervention, my younger sister, Kristina, and I were actually removed from our biological parents' home and placed in an orphanage run by Protestant nuns. Kristina was only two years old at the time, and I was three.

It's difficult to convey the atmosphere of this institution and its nuns back then in Germany. In those days, an orphanage was simply a prison for children. We were isolated from the world. All we could know about the world outside of our orphanage/prison walls was what we saw on television and heard on the radio. Even these outlets were strictly supervised and minimal. We were allowed to watch TV only on Sunday. I still remember the shows we watched: *Rin-Tin-Tin*, *Fury*, and *Lassie*, all of them American shows. I was glued to the television, its small screen broadcasting in black-and-white, fascinated by the freedom these fictional children had. Big refrigerators with food in them, available to the children whenever they wanted something to eat! Something I could only dream about. At the orphanage, we had only breakfast, lunch, and dinner, with nothing in between. No snacks certainly, and dessert not very often.

Those fictional children had big yards and neighborhoods to play in; we had a walled-off courtyard that was small and not really conducive to children playing in it. Those fictional children had pets, cats and dogs and birds that, again, we orphans had no hope of having.

Fortunately for my younger sister, she was soon adopted by an American couple. We were separated when she went to live with them in the United States. How could they have done that to us? She was my only close family member.

I was too young to understand what was going on; all I knew was that she was gone one day. Both of us had blonde hair and blue eyes; however, my sister was a tad lighter than me, a trait the American couple was looking for because the wife had blonde hair and blue eyes. They wanted a child who looked more like her.

Over the years, I never forgot my sister and kept asking for her. When I was about ten years old, one of the nuns finally told me that she was adopted and that I would never see her again. It was like a slap in the face.

Why her? Why not me? There was not a day that I did not think of her. I remember at night I used to look up to the stars and moon, and I told myself, "These are the same stars and the same moon Kristina is seeing, right now, wherever she is." It gave me some comfort knowing that she saw them as well.

How I envied her, for I thought she had the life I always dreamed of, the life I only knew through the televisions shows. I used to imagine that I was Timmy, the boy who played in Lassie, having all the freedom he had and a caring mom. I was convinced that my sister had a life like this, and oh, how I envied her! "I will find her one day!" This was a promise I made to myself.

In fact, during my childhood, I was trundled off

to a succession of four or five orphanages because they were categorized according to age. The first orphanage was for babies, then toddlers, and so on. One thing all the orphanages had in common was an extremely regimented, militaristic way of life. We were children but received no affection, no kind words, encouragement, or praise as we were growing up. The system was strict beyond all reason. Being told each day what to do and how to live your life was pure hell, and I personally found it especially hard being told what to wear.

Since I was a real tomboy, I loved pants, but the only time we were allowed to wear pants was when we went sledding. Every Sunday, we had to go to church, dressed in gray and walking two and two behind each other (an apron-like over-garment), which made us all look like girls from the TV show *Little House on the Prairie*. How I hated it because it identified us as the little orphans, which meant those sorrowful-looking eyes glued on us. It made me wish I could disappear. It gave me the feeling of a punishment because we were orphaned.

I remember desperately trying not to look up, my eyes pinned to the ground so I didn't have to see the faces. This was the moment when I envied my sister who was adopted and was not exposed to such cruelty. Yes, I can honestly say the word cruelty, because this is what it felt like as a child.

Freedom, I want freedom, was the thought in my mind, and it could not—would not—be erased. At night, I used to cover myself with my blanket so no one could hear me repeating my name over and over again. It was a voice most familiar to me, like the voice of a mother to her child, and since I had no mother of my own, I pacified myself with my own voice till I finally fell asleep. Life in the orphanage was all about being told no, always being on the defensive, and being commanded what to do all the time. In bed at eight, up in the morning at seven, lunch precisely at noon, and so on.

As I already mentioned, I was a tomboy, but girls were not allowed to wear any kind of pants or jeans. Always a dress, and our hair had to be braided, not loose. None of my childhood memories were good; none of the orphanages were pleasant.

I recall a particularly monstrous episode; it's a very vivid memory I can't erase.

I must have been about three years old. Every day around noon, all the children were put down for a nap. All the cribs were right next to each other. One sunny day, I just did not feel like taking a nap. As I stood up in my crib, I noticed a small shelf with toys on it at a wall nearby. As I grasped one of the toys, the child in the crib next to me got up as well. He was trying to grab the toy out of my hand.

Of course, as children do, we got into a little skirmish, and our squeals and crying prompted one of the nuns to rush into the room and over to us. She wrested the toy from me, lifted me up, and carried me outdoors to the patio where all the other nuns were sitting, passing the time knitting or reading. On the side of the patio sat a big wooden box. She proceeded to the box, opened it, placed me inside, and then closed the cover.

The box had a few holes on the side. I remember lying on my stomach looking out of the holes, watching the nuns. I must have fallen asleep or gone unconscious just to cope with the shock of feeling buried alive. I do not remember being taken out. I was three years old!

And of course I had no rights. The nuns were

in charge, and that was the designated punishment for me: incarceration in an enclosed wooden box, much like a coffin, dark and terrifying. Throughout my childhood years, in and out of one harrowing orphanage after another, a singular goal controlled my young mind: escape! The feeling of being trapped was present every day. How I longed to be free and away from each dreaded prison.

I remember having a recurring dream of breaking out. In my dream, I had wings and was able to fly over the walls that isolated me from the outside world. I could see myself flying away by just lifting my arms. In the dream, I could reach up in the air, and yet I was not moving. I was trapped. To me, the world on the other side of those walls meant freedom. The dream haunted me for years, even into young adulthood.

So, from the age of three until age eighteen, I grew up in different orphanages in postwar Germany, totally isolated from the outside world other than those Sunday church visits, which were in a regular church outside the walls. Today, reflecting on my childhood years, I am 100 percent convinced that if I had the love, caring, and security of a loving family, it would have helped me accept the changes in later life and would have given me greater strength in dealing with the obstacles of aging and life itself.

At age eighteen, after I was released from the last orphanage, I quickly met my future husband, a soldier in the US Army. We were in housing provided by the military, and there we lived with many other young military families. This will be hard to believe, but I thought that America was populated exclusively by young people. I guess it was because of all the American soldiers and their families, all who were young.

Later, when I immigrated to the United States, I was surprised to see people of all different ages! Talking to other friends who also came here at a young age, they seem to agree with me on this. It is evidence that when you see only one thing, you start to believe in that image, that notion; we think it's the way it really is. So my concern is that children today who are being taught that being beautiful is of primary importance will have a difficult time accepting otherwise.

It brings to mind a perverse curiosity I discovered while channel surfing. It's a television show called *Toddlers and Tiaras* about real people who enter their children in beauty pageants. In this beauty pageant world, very young children are learning to be competitive about looking beautiful and staying beautiful. If you haven't seen the show, you might be shocked to discover that these pageants include infants as young as eight months old!

There are various divisions based on age groupings, and parents seem to be living vicariously through their children. For the children, it's like a rehearsal of the wrong message over and over. A recipe for disaster? Should we be surprised if these kids grow up with identity problems, having been programmed in skin-deep values? They have been drilled all their lives that their most important role in society is to be a fake version of beauty. You must look sexy, wear makeup, and act as grown-up as possible.

Of course, these shows aren't the only symptoms; there are many shows with overemphasis on making over various people and places, or survivor-type shows, all emphasizing appearance, physical prowess, and nasty behavior to other people. With the exception of *Jeopardy*, there's little on television that emphasizes intellectual achievement.

One last incident reinforced to me the notion of Hollywood calling for a youthful appearance.

Two years ago, I bought a pale pink scooter, not a motorcycle but a type of motorbike. I love riding it, usually in the warmer months. Breezing around in the open air is exhilarating and lots of fun. But I want to mention the extra perk I experience whenever I'm riding through town. I get so much attention! Not only from men but kids, boys and girls too—they all call out to me, comments like "Cool bike!" and "Go, girl!" with thumbs up.

At red lights, people ask me about the scooter, where I bought it, things like that. You see, I've always been petite and wear size 0–2. Under my helmet and fashionable sunglasses, what people see is a slender female body in jeans on a small, feminine version of a Harley. No wonder compliments are flying!

Whenever this happens I have to smile to myself. I imagine how my admirers might react if I called back, "Let me take my helmet off. Look a little closer. I'm not the twenty-year-old hottie you think you see!" But I never take my helmet off. I opt for the fun, favorable attention, however temporary.

Yes, popular culture and Hollywood can wield a lot of power over many women, oppressive power. Impossible demands. Could I be totally satisfied with myself, I pondered, even as time kept marching on? I resolved to do whatever it took to comply—that is, to stay young looking and succumb to their shallow terms. It was my choice to keep identifying with youthful attractiveness, and I was determined to keep battling this unwinnable war.

What a mistake.

Chapter 4

DR. CHARM: THE NIGHTMARE PARAMOUR

ODDLY ENOUGH, THE pressure to start my anti-aging battle began when I was in my twenties.

It was the mid to late 1970s. I was about twenty-five years old and already divorced from my soldier husband after only eight years of marriage. I was also on the verge of becoming a workaholic while working for a travel agency in Bay Shore, New York.

An amiable friend of mine who knew I was single again called me up one day. Anthony was a physician who worked in a hospital nearby. "Victoria, how's it going?" Anthony's voice was warm; he was always outgoing and upbeat.

We chatted for a little while.

Eventually, he asked, "Do you think you might be interested in going out with a friend of mine? He's also a colleague, a doctor who works here at the hospital."

That took me by surprise! I must have gasped slightly, which he interpreted as an invitation to start teasing me about working too much and being too serious.

"Word is out, Victoria. You're in danger of catching the all-work-and-no-play syndrome. Hmm … it's a disorder characterized by working too many hours while neglecting your social life. You don't want to be one of those people who never has any fun, do you?" By this time, Anthony was obviously amused at his clever ploy.

"I have fun," I protested.

"Not enough," he replied. "My prescription for you? You need to meet my doctor friend as a preventive measure. So you won't become a worker drone who's no fun to be with anymore. You know what they say—that a doctor is catnip to a woman the way a model is to a man. By the way, he is good-looking."

"Oh, Anthony, you know what they say about good-looking men. They're not one-woman men, and to top it off, he's a doctor? They never have problems finding women. I am not too sure if I even want to go this direction."

At this, Anthony laughed. He told me his friend's name was John and that John had been married twice and was in his early forties but had no children. Although two divorces raised a minor red flag in my mind, I was persuaded. I agreed to Anthony's attempt at matchmaking.

A few days later, my phone rang. Doctor John introduced himself. His voice was nice, and he sounded like he was a genuinely likable guy. He briefly described himself as tall, a little over six feet, black hair, not too short but not too long, medium build, hazel eyes, regular features, and very fit.

"Are you being modest?" I asked. "According to Anthony, you're good-looking." Yes, I was flirting a little because he really did come across, on the phone anyway, as a nice guy. Maybe he was trying to impress me by not being conceited.

He laughed and said, "Well you know how friends are. I guess you could say I'm reasonably attractive."

It worked. He impressed me as a down-to-earth

man sincerely interested in meeting a nice, attractive woman for friendship, as a companion to go out with, to enjoy good times and then see where it might go. No pressure. Then I offered a brief description of myself (modestly, of course), at which he suggested that I'm prettier than I was admitting. *Hmm*, I thought, *smooth but sweet.*

We made a date to meet the next evening at an upscale bar/restaurant near the hospital. I was still very young, on the green side of twenty-three, and he was much more sophisticated, a worldly man who had just entered middle age. But because I was so young and had married at such a young age, I lacked the perspective that a women with more dating experience would have had. The truth is this was a time in my life that I hate to remember. I fact, I deliberately blocked it out of my mind as best as I could after it ended.

Many years later, I hardly think about it anymore. However, it's important to include the story of my relationship with John because it was fundamental in laying the groundwork for my subsequent aging complex, what I've come to label as my fear-of-aging disorder. In hindsight all these years later, I realize this. Hard as it is for me to talk about, this sordid episode needs to be told.

After Anthony's call, I considered that all I knew about John was that he was a doctor, good-looking (according to Anthony), and had two marriages behind him. My thoughts swirled with anticipation, wondering why John's ex-wives divorced him. And if he was such a catch, why was there no woman in his life now? *But*, I reasoned, *maybe that's why—maybe he doesn't want to make another mistake in the relationship department.* Okay, that made sense to my youthful mind. *Well*, I thought, *tomorrow I'll see for myself, and my questions will be answered.*

The next day, I was abuzz with anticipation. At six o'clock after a long day's work, I walked into the neighborhood place we'd agreed on. I headed over to the bar area. A few people were already there enjoying drinks and conversation. Based on John's description of himself, I had an idea of what to look for. However, there were several men sitting at the bar with similar features, like dark brown hair and so forth. I studied each one of them until my eyes fell on one who had a profile like a movie star. As I got closer and I could see more of his face, my heart did a thump-thump. This man was not merely good-looking; he was drop-dead gorgeous. *Oh please*, I thought, *let it be him!*

At that moment, Mr. Movie Star Profile turned around from his perch at the bar. His eyes met mine with a small half smile. Then I knew. It was John. He was so handsome it took my breath away. I was speechless except for my thoughts—*tall, dark, and handsome*. A girl's dream. The fact that he was almost twenty years older than I was at the time didn't bother me in the least. Not with looks like that.

"What are you drinking?" he asked after we introduced ourselves. His eyes were attentive, almost circumspect. Pulling out a bar-stool for me to sit next to him, his manner was comfortable and assured but not cocky. In minutes, we were engrossed in conversation. He told me about his area of specialization at the hospital.

"Chief of surgery in the OR? How terrifying!" It sounded enormously exciting and intimidating to me. My work experience was confined to clerical tasks and office jobs. The thought of blood at work made me nervous.

He laughed. Apparently it wasn't the first time he had experienced my kind of reaction to his responsibilities in the operating room. The operating room! "It's true that I do make some life and death decisions. But usually they're routine procedures like appendectomies, gall stones, things like that, you know?"

Honestly, I couldn't imagine working in a hospital, so I was pretty fascinated listening to him. Likewise, he was fascinated by my European background. Or so I thought. (The real reason for his interest, I would find out later.) But at this, our first meeting, I believed there was something about me he liked and that he was sincere in wanting to know me better. We had no trouble talking some more. There were no awkward breaks or halting conversations that are so common on first dates.

Time passed until we noticed the bar was getting less and less crowded, and we decided to wrap up our evening. As we got ready to leave, he asked me for a second date. Of course, I accepted.

What followed was a whirlwind romance, something I'd never experienced before. We were out and about several nights a week as John showed me some wonderful times and spent money freely. He was all about charm. Yes, he could be so charming that my secret, unspoken nickname was Dr. Charm. He lavished attention on me, which made me feel wonderful and significant.

Looking back now, of course I understand I was coming from a bereft childhood, growing up in an unloving, sterile orphanage. No one paid much attention to me. No one ever said I was pretty, smart, or worthwhile. In post–World War II Germany, being an orphan was to be a child with a number rather than a name. Everything about orphanage life was militaristic and stripped of identity, individuality, and any sense of fun or freedom.

All of which is to say I was exceptionally vulnerable to John's attentiveness. About a month later, in the midst of being romanced and swept off my feet, John asked me to move in with him. It was disconcerting to say the least. My surprise was obvious.

"My house is big, Victoria. You know that. Being there alone, um … it's not good to live alone. I know I could make you feel at home there. With me."

"We've only been together a few weeks."

"I know. But just think about it. Okay?"

I don't remember having to convince myself for very long before I said yes. Accepting his offer was the wrong choice and the biggest mistake of my life. Plaques, credentials, and awards lined a wall in his study in his beautiful home, a rambling ranch with four bedrooms and one whole bathroom upstairs. Downstairs was a large living room, another bathroom, a den, and a beautiful kitchen overlooking the backyard, which looked like a small park. And yes, he was an accomplished doctor, without a doubt. His grand house was a testimony to his success. But his diplomas and awards were not evidence that he was a great person.

Soon after I'd settled into my new, luxurious environment, our whirlwind romance devolved into a routine in which my role was exposed: I was his live-in sex partner, housekeeper, cook, laundress, and all-around personal assistant. I did everything for this man—all the shopping, all the housework, all the scut work entailed in running a home, still having a full-time job in New York City!

He expected it, as if nothing could be more normal. Dr. Charm evaporated, and Dr. Despot emerged. All the while he was ruling over the house and me in it, he still perceived himself as Dr. Charm. It confused me. His extreme good looks and professional status entitled him, to his way of thinking, to royal treatment. He thought women should cater to him, cooking after he returned home in the evening from work, making sure his suits were picked up from the cleaners, keeping the house clean, and so on …

Again, my youth and inexperience were the factors I attribute to my meek acceptance of my lowly status and his exalted one. How I regretted moving in with him! Looking back on our whirlwind romance, I could see more clearly. He was a man who would say anything to get a woman in bed. And he was good at it. Although I somehow went along with fulfilling the role designated for me, of course I was unhappy. And it got worse. Living with him, other elements of his personality were revealed that were perverse. During our fleeting romance, he had succeeded in deceiving me because I could not have imagined his sick inclinations that would come out later.

At the time, I was close friends with a nineteen-year-old girl, Lisa, who used to work in the same office that I did. Sometimes we'd go to a movie or meet for lunch or coffee. One time she came over to the house—John's house—to visit me. She was a lovely young woman, opposite in appearance to me. While I was blonde, blue eyed, and petite, Lisa was slim with long, dark brown hair and hazel eyes.

"What's going on, Victoria?" she asked.

"What do you mean?"

"I know something's wrong. Ever since you moved in here. I thought you were excited about living with John."

"Well, it's not exactly how I thought it would be. It's kind of hard. Umm, I mean, adjusting, you know?" It was embarrassing to me. I didn't want her to know that I had made such a stupid mistake, moving in with a man I dated for only a month.

"That's probably normal. But this house! Maybe you should—"

Her words were interrupted when Dr. John himself strolled in, smiling. I introduced him to

Lisa. After saying, "Nice to meet you," John went upstairs.

"Wow, he's so handsome. Even better looking than I pictured him. Even though he's old enough to be my father—and almost old enough to be yours too. Hey, is that it? Are you having trouble because of the age difference?"

"No, it's not that. It's just different now than when we were dating."

The truth is it was not just the servile life as personal assistant / sex partner that had me feeling down and blue. He was a cheater. An open cheater, meaning he didn't bother to hide his flings and one-night stands from me because, after all, he reminded me snidely, "We're not married."

Midlife crisis is a real phenomenon for many people. But at age twenty-five, I had no frame of reference for this stage he was going through. I still had most of my life ahead of me. Nor did I know that sex addiction is real, that there are many individuals who live with this disorder. Like any addict, a heroin junkie, a compulsive gambler, or even a person who can't quit cigarettes, a sex addict is driven to satisfy his addiction. Sex was the centerpiece of John's life. The sex obsession that framed his life was Dr. Charm's secret.

He kept his secret from any new woman in his life for as long as he possibly could. It began to make sense to me that he hurried our romance and rushed his invitation to live with him before I discovered his secret. Having a women around was essential to his lifestyle, and I fit the bill at that time. Countless nights, I was awakened by him getting in bed after being out, doing who knows what with who knows who.

He tried to cajole me into the lifestyle. "What about it? You're adventurous. Aren't you? Take my word for it; it's a natural high. A sensual high."

"No." No. That was all I could manage to say. I was thunderstruck. He asked me to join him and another woman in a sexual threesome. Sometime soon, like this weekend? A sexual triad was not in my repertoire, nor had I ever thought about such debauchery.

But that wasn't the worst of it. His need for sex was enormous, and he had an eye for very young women, even younger than I was in my early twenties. I was young and pretty, and my youth was a reason for his attraction to me, it's true. But he was also a master of deceit about his propensities, ones he kept hidden from me while we merely dated. Propensities, I soon learned, that were beyond the pale.

One morning about two months after I'd moved in, we were having breakfast. It was about a week after I had casually introduced him to Lisa. He looked at me over his cup of coffee. "Victoria, I was wondering, would you mind fixing me up with your friend Lisa?"

He flat out asked me to arrange for him to have sex with my nineteen-year-old friend! He was forty-two and actually proceeded to tell me about his fantasies to be with very young girls! As if it was a common, acceptable topic for conversation.

"What?" The spoon in my hand dropped to the table. "How can you ask me that?"

"What's the big deal? I asked a simple question."

"There's no way I could ask my teenage friend to go out with you, John."

His condescending gaze cut worse than his words. "Forget it!"

He stood up and left for the hospital. Did I just hear what I thought I heard? Did he really ask me to pimp my friend to him? Repulsed, I rose from the table and ran to the bathroom. I stared at my face in the mirror. I'm ashamed to confess that, despite the perversion of his question, I was instantly worried about my appearance. Yes, I was young, especially compared to his early middle age. But apparently not young enough. My head was spinning. *I'm young! But does this mean I'm getting old?*

Panicking, I studied every inch of my face in search of a line, a flaw. *Is there a big difference between a nineteen-year-old's looks and a twenty-three-year-old's looks? Four years!* Another thing I didn't realize back then was that the issue wasn't really appearance. How much older could I possibly look, being only four years older than Lisa?

The issue for him was chronology. The attraction for him was about how young the girl was. After all, he'd just casually told me—after I'd been living in his house—about his fantasies to have sex with young girls. Or at least as young as he could get away with. In fact, it didn't even matter if the girl was particularly attractive or not. What mattered was her age, the younger the better. But I didn't understand this at the time.

All I felt was a rude disruption in my senses about my own attractiveness. A seed had been planted from which my obsession about aging would grow. And flourish. Doubts about my desirability was born, all because I interpreted his perverted sexual inclination to mean I was already getting old. Naive? Yes, I was. Inexperienced and vulnerable, his view had an impact on me. It started my fight against getting old. At age twenty-three!

For all intents and purposes he was a repugnant pedophile. Yet from that day on, every chance I had to be alone, I'd study my face in the mirror. There were not, however, many days and nights I hung around after that. Was this the kind of man I really wanted to be with? At the beginning, I liked him and believed we would have a great relationship. That was before I learned about the vile sexual world he was in. Whatever happened, I knew I could not and would not want to stay with him.

A week of sleepless nights later, I decided to leave him, knowing it was the right decision. Staring at the alarm clock every night, all night long, it was a relief that he was not beside me in bed. I was relieved he was out whoring around because I could not stand to have him touch me again. An urgency took charge of me, an urgent need to get away from him, as far away as possible. Away from him, away from the unsavory memories, away from the miserable life as housekeeper and sex partner. His troublesome request to be fixed up with Lisa had shocked me back into my own moral world where I could see clearly again: this was a man wholly unclean in his mind and soul.

Germany! That's where I would go to get far away from him, where he would not come after me. I needed space to breathe again. I needed time to recover from the damage of so many indignities, from the prison his house had become to me. My job allowed me to have my own income, which gave me some independence. I had already canceled my lease on the apartment I had before I moved in with John. I'd also sold most of the furniture and gave the rest to friends. I was able to put away enough money to start over again in a new place.

I once read a small note written by Erich Fried (1921–1988). It said: "For the world you are just someone, but for someone you will be the world." With this in mind, I was ready for the next step. Leaving Dr. John was more of an escape than a trip. I could not wait to put this interlude in my life in the past and keep it there. Physical distance would do that. As I mentioned earlier, this is a time in my life I hate to remember. I don't know how to end this chapter except to say my escape to Germany afforded some temporary relief. I was able to wash the unclean memories from my soul. But the nightmare of age obsession had only just begun.

Chapter 5

ESCAPE FROM THE NIGHTMARE

AFTER LEAVING JOHN, I prepared myself to leave for Germany. I picked up my daughter, Valentina, who was five years old at the time and who was staying with her father after our divorce, to take her back with me to Germany.

Only a few months later, as I got settled halfway into my new life, restlessness got a hold of me, when I made a split-second decision about moving back to Germany. Whatever little I bought to set up a home was sold, and with my daughter in tow, I returned to New York. This journey was repeated three more times. I could not get settled and had an inner restlessness that was not easy to shake.

On one of my returns to Germany, I remember

very vividly I had a window seat. Looking out of the window, I felt so empty. Over and over I kept asking myself, "Vicky, what do you really want? You cannot keep flying back and forth. Make up your mind!" Tears were running down my checks, which felt good; it felt like a relief valve was opened to let out the pressure that was building up in me. My restlessness felt so raw, and there was nothing I could do about it.

Valentina was going to start school soon. I had to come to a final decision. I had to find that inner peace. Soon after my arrival in Germany, I was lucky enough to find a small furnished apartment and a job with an insurance company. I was turning over a new leaf, and the time away from a place that gave me so much misery was a welcome change. I registered my daughter in a German nursery. Children in Germany start school when they are six years old. Valentina was only five years old and not eligible yet. I was able to drop her of before leaving for work and pick her up in the evening on my way home.

Before long, we both settled into our new life. One morning as I got ready for work and was just about to leave, by the front door I noticed on the floor a small bag with a real flower on top of the bag. A little surprised, I picked up the little bag to see what was in it. I found a small note that said, "Enjoy your breakfast!" No name or any other indication where it came from. Inside were two fresh-baked rolls still somehow warm, which only could mean that they were fresh out of the oven. This happened a few more times and always with a fresh flower on top of the bag ...

Then on a weekend, I thought I heard someone by my door. I opened it, and to my surprise, there was a man about seven years my senior. He then introduced himself as Klaus, and he was a neighbor from one flight up. I introduced myself.

"I've been putting the bag of rolls here for you. I leave for work about an hour before you, so when I go to the bakery around the corner for breakfast, I get two extra ones for you two."

"Thank you. That's nice of you to be so considerate." We had some more small talk, and he told me that he was watching me from his bedroom window the day I moved in.

In his conversation, he also mentioned that his hobby was his paddle boat. He belonged to a club where everyone had one, and on weekends or holidays, they met at different rivers to race down to the end of the river. "Oh this sounds so adventurous!" I said.

"Yes, it sure is," he answered. "If you ever feel up to it, you and your daughter are more than welcome to come. I have a camper. There is more than enough room for us three."

I gladly accepted his offer. This was the beginning of a brand-new adventure and friendship. From that day on, almost every weekend and holiday, we packed up the camper to explore a new river. The club had about twenty members, some of them with families and children, which gave Valentina plenty of friends to play with.

We used to meet at the campground near the river. At night, we sat around a bonfire to talk about the day and plan our agenda for the next day. We used to meet at rivers not only in Germany but places like France, Austria, and even Italy, countries that bordered Germany or were only a few hours away by car.

I remember one particular campground in the mountains of Southern France. Every morning, not even a mile away, a shepherd brought his sheep to feed on the grass, and toward the evening, they returned back home. It was music to our ears to hear them coming up the mountain every morning.

I have some great memories of this time. I was in Germany for about nine months when I realized I had to return to the United States. As a green card holder, I was not allowed to stay more than one year away from the States without taking the chance of losing my privileges as an immigrant. Valentina was a US citizen, I had no worries on that end, but for me it was a different story.

With a heavy heart, I started to make arrangement for my trip back to the States. Another reason for returning was Valentina's family—her grandma, uncles, aunts, and cousins—were all there, something I did not want to take away from her.

In Klaus I found a wonderful friend. Even today, our friendship continues more than forty years later. Whenever I visit Germany, I am always welcome in his house. Yes, over the years I have met wonderful partners/friends, but I just could not bring myself to another commitment, which meant being restricted.

On my return to the States, I finally decided to buy a house. I was tired of not having a home to call my own. Deciding to get a house of my own took a while, as it meant being tied down and having responsibilities I wasn't sure I was ready for. Not a perfect time when I still had that desire to be free. I also felt I owed it to my daughter to have a place she could call home, to give her some stability after our many moves back and forth between two continents.

A few months later, I seemed to find what I was searching for, a nice four-bedroom home in a suburb of NYC, about eight miles from the open Atlantic. I was ready to start my life over again, like so many times before, and hoped this would be the last time.

Chapter 6

THE ONE WHO GOT AWAY

LIFE CAN BE both dreadful and wonderful. In the early 1980s, I moved back to the United States permanently, bought a house, and resettled into American life. I was about forty years old, but I had a lot to learn.

"Where should we go?" Brit said impatiently to me one night. She was in overdrive mode.

We'd been friends for three years, since I'd been introduced to her by a coworker. We seemed to hit it off right away and had many things in common; we both liked happy hour, meeting new people, traveling, and so on.

Brit was my best friend. Initially blessed with a happy marriage, Brit had been prematurely widowed years ago. Accustomed to having a supportive man in her life, she was constantly on the lookout for a new someone, not for a fling but for a commitment. Vivacious and cute, she was petite like me, only with a few extra pounds and shoulder-length brown hair.

She also dressed a little on the sexy side, and men were easily attracted to her. She had no problem meeting and dating them. It was her aggressive marriage mindedness that invariably scared them away. Meanwhile, she was currently embroiled in a clandestine entanglement with a wealthy married man.

When it came to happy hour on Friday, she meant business. We were meeting at our usual Place in Hauppauge, NY, a cozy little bar surrounded by office buildings, which also meant a chance of meeting white-collar people. Ever on the prowl for attractive, eligible men, she took charge of researching the current "hot" places where her preferred species congregated after work: men with means. At the time, I was a young forty, divorced, and working in the typical office environment. Mostly I just went along for the ride.

The After Hours Grill was living up to its

reputation as the place to be for a Friday happy hour. Top-shelf cocktails, dusky lit atmosphere, and casual-chic surroundings were just sexy enough to cut loose after a long week. And maybe something more. Like romantic possibilities for patrons so inclined.

Brit and I maneuvered our way through the crowd to the bar. She ordered her usual merlot, and I my Baileys on the rocks. Admittedly, I'm not much of a drinker, but Baileys is almost as good as a milkshake.

Brit swallowed down a good slug of her drink, then turned to me, continuing our discussion— our endless discussion—about her latest beau. "I know I've got to break it off." A pause. "But, Vicky, he treats me like a princess! And we have so much fun."

"Brit, you know he's not going to leave his wife. For a woman who wants to get married again? Honestly, Brit, you've known this from the beginning! It's a dead end."

The Grill was standing room only by now, the clatter of alcohol-enhanced conversation buzzing around us.

"I know, I know. Okay. Let's drink to meeting

new people. A new man in your life too." Her toast was about to come true. What happened next could not possibly have been planned or predicted.

"Das project duerfte nicht laenger als ein paar wochen dauern."

My ears perked up. Somewhere over the noise and flirting going on around the room, I heard a man speaking in German! Who knows German in a happy hour bar in Hauppauge, New York? But there it was again. Someone had just said, "The project should not take longer than a few weeks." Snippets of words here and there, male voices were conversing in my first language. I turned my head, intrigued. Scrutinizing the immediate vicinity, my gaze stopped at a particular table.

Seated not too far away, four men's verbal exchanges were definitely in German, exclusively in German. Now this I had to investigate.

"I'll be back in a minute," I promised Brit, and walked over to their table. "Was bringt euch hier in die USA?" Smiling, I addressed the gentlemen collectively. ("What brings you here to the USA?")

"Oh, du sprichtst auch deutsch?" ("Oh, you speak German as well?") The youngest member of their party, handsome with dark blond hair and a chiseled face, responded with friendly surprise. As we chatted for a minute or two, it was generally established that all of us had the same idea—to relax, to finish the week with drinks and genial conversation. I was impressed to learn that the four men were highly positioned engineers on a temporary two-year work assignment at a nearby firm.

"Join us! Bring your friend over." They were an outgoing group, and Brit couldn't have been more pleased at their invitation. "What are you drinking?"

Another round of Baileys and merlot for Brit and me, while the men were committed to their scotch. Wineglass in hand, Brit proceeded to charm them all as she embarked on her undercover mission: find out who, among this glorious testosterone- filled circle, was single or divorced and therefore a prospective new partner.

Meanwhile, the fiftysomething fellow seemed to have eyes only for me. Classic looking and dashing in his Armani suit, he made deliberate eye contact with me. "Wie schoen von jemand so angenehm angesprochen zu werden in einer

Stadt wie Hauppauge." ("What a nice surprise, to be approached by someone so pleasant in a town like Hauppauge.")

And with that, we were riveted to each other for the rest of the evening. Both of us intent on knowing the other quickly and completely, time became irrelevant. We talked and kept on talking. It was mutual captivation.

"Heaven must have sent you here tonight, Victoria. Here I am, all alone and new in town. Did I mention I've only been here a week?" He was being faux coy.

Cute, I thought. His name was Werner. A manicured beard and mustache trimmed his face, which, though refined, kept a boyish hint. His urbane manner and almost macho confidence were alluring. As our conversation progressed, his words were accompanied by small touches. His hand over my hand, a fleeting touch on my shoulder.

The questions he asked me—Where am I to go? What is there to do for amusement?—made me feel like an experienced native. He smiled at me. "You're needed, Victoria! You are appointed to be my guide. You lead. I'll follow."

Eventually his right arm found its way across my back, his hand resting on my right shoulder. Not that I objected. I was wearing a Baileys glow by then. Doing my own share of flirting, I added small fleeting touches too ... my hand on his arm, on his hand. I learned he was divorced and had two grown children, both in college. He was proud of them, his son an engineering student, his daughter in art history. His remarkable career swept him all over the world, and he had lived in exotic places including South Africa and the Middle East. I envied him for that.

"How thrilling to experience so many different cultures." Fortunately for me, he enjoyed talking about them and answering my many questions. Three hours flew by. I announced my intention to head home.

"But I won't let you leave without giving me your phone number."

If he had only known. There was no way on earth I would have left the Grill that night without making sure he had my phone number! After my own divorce a decade before, Werner was the first man I met who I was honestly interested in spending time with. That he was twelve years older than I was actually enhanced his attractiveness. He was irresistible. Maybe he knew it. And our meeting was pure serendipity!

We kept in touch on a regular basis, calling each other or meeting for a drink whenever possible.

"Can I entice you with a fine lobster dinner, as prepared for you by me, Chef Werner?" he asked me on one of our phone conversations. Could he, indeed! It was our third date. Werner, I soon discovered, was a gifted "hobby" cook. At our first meeting when we talked for hours, I had disclosed my enthusiasm for seafood, especially lobster. He had assured me that he was an excellent amateur cook. I had impudently replied that I would be the judge of that.

That evening at his apartment, my verdict was in: "Yes. You are an excellent cook!" Without a doubt, his was the choicest lobster dinner I had ever eaten. This is not hyperbole but absolutely true.

Every single time he ever cooked for me, the food was amazing! He was incredibly inventive with it too. Even from leftovers he would concoct impromptu appetizers that were out of this world.

I preferred Werner's home-cooked gourmet meals over any fancy restaurant. During the weeks and months that followed, our relationship deepened in intensity, and sexual intimacy was added to the menu. Our physical synergy was breathtaking. It was a form of passion I didn't know before being with him.

Weeks and months went by, and each time we met, it was clear to me Werner was most certainly a man I enjoyed spending time with. Six months after we first met, my moment of questioning finally arrived. The forbidden thought entered my mind: is he someone I want to be with for the rest of my life? No matter what we were doing, we took so much pleasure in each others company.

One of my favorite things about spending time with Werner was listening to his stories. For hours I would listen, mesmerized, to his anecdotes of exotic places where his work had taken him: South Africa, China, South America, Iran, and Pakistan, to name some of them. This was many years prior to September 11, 2001, of course, and travel and access was easier in those times. At these locales, he had always lived in gated communities. People from the Western countries who had temporary assignments in the Middle East were kept isolated due to the difference in culture.

His stories of the Middle East were exciting. I felt like a child witnessing the *Tales of the Arabian Nights* leap off the page into real life—his life. A born storyteller, Werner never failed to enthrall me. But sometimes his experiences of life in the Middle East elicited my protests. Aversion even. For example, scorpions, anyone? Do you think you would sleep well at night knowing you were not alone? Because your nocturnal visitors ambling around your bedroom floor might be scorpions! Envision deep, coffee-sized cans filled with kerosene oil, strategically placed to hold your bedposts. Why? The cans of oil function as your moat, your protection from those scorpions creeping their way into your bed!

Werner said matter-of-factually, "When I woke up in the morning, I'd see dead scorpions drowned in oil. They fell to their gooey liquid death as they attempted to crawl up onto the bed by way of the bedposts." Poor creatures, they were helpless to climb out of their tin, slippery prisons. Ugh! It was an image too alien and terrifying for me.

Werner's adventuresome spirit and spontaneity were magnetic. Werner was an individual who did things out of the ordinary. There were times at the beginning of a long holiday weekend when he'd startle me—in a good way—with an abrupt suggestion like, "Let's go to the Bahamas!" No matter where we went on our weekend excursions, we never took the tourist route, never did things the typical way. No, Werner was a man of the world and believed in going native. Wherever tourists don't go, we did go.

One time, Haiti was the weekend island we went to visit. To get to know the island better, we decided to rent a car, which enabled us to visit local outdoor markets, shop, and eat what the people who lived there were eating—fresh fish, fruit, and vegetables. We even ventured up into the mountains where we saw indigenous people living in hutches, sleeping on the floors. Crowds of squealing children surrounded us as we gave them lollipops and other candy to their sweet delight. Evenings we spent by the beach, where we sat in the sand, watching the sun set, Werner often telling me about his time in foreign countries.

Werner was a master storyteller. This strange desert episode really happened, he insisted, one evening when he was living in Iran. Watching his face as he recounted the unseemly tale, I could see he was reliving the moment. "It was like a dream," he said.

"It had become a frequent habit of mine," Werner continued his story, "after work to jump into my sand buggy and jet out—out into the desert ... to solitude. To clear my mind, to leave every concern, every responsibility, ever conflict and problem behind me. Just let me forget! Let me be uncultivated, wild ... a part of the environment, like a cactus that doesn't need care, that doesn't care, that has no cares ... That's all I wanted, and the desert seduced me. Escape ...

"One evening, it was twilight, the sun finishing its slide down, down. To my shock, I saw I wasn't the only person in the desert that night. Night was cued to make its entrance, a breathtaking vision. Always, when I began these getaways, it was unbearably hot ... a sensual heat ... a punishing heat. But by the time I traveled deep into that sand sanctuary, it got colder and colder. So many people think a desert is perpetual heat.

But the truth is, after a time, around twilight, the temperature plummets. It gets cool, then cooler. By midnight, if you stick around long enough, the temperature dwindles down to single digits.

"This time, I saw a figure in the far distance on horseback. Fascinated, I drove closer, maintaining enough space between myself and my unexpected company. It was a woman! Naked. With no saddle to encumber her steed, her lithe body silhouetted against the sky. The profile of her face was trailed by her own mane of hair, overflowing, lavish. She flew past me. Straight ahead, transfixed, then further away … Passing by in the far distance. Like the sun, her horse slid down … then out of sight."

During that period of his life, he was in the midst of a difficult marriage. With his wife and two small children in a foreign culture, on a portion of the globe so wholly different from their native Germany, it was an adventure to him. For his wife, it was not. I never asked questions about his (now) ex-wife, because I didn't want to pry. He scattered spare clues here and there that indicated a tumultuous situation at home and a small glimpse of his personal unhappiness.

His explanation of the incident, seeing the young native Iranian woman galloping naked in a trancelike state of freedom was, I thought, parallel to his life at that time.

He explained that the oppressive culture was extremely harsh on women. They were required to be robed, completely covered from head to foot, on a daily basis. His own wife had to "robe up" before going out, to avoid causing trouble. This despite the fact that they were Western visitors residing in a gated community. Returning to his earnest reasoning, he believed the young woman was out in the desert alone, speeding by horseback to escape, however temporarily, the excessive constraints she was forced to endure every day of her life.

Did it really happen? Werner, without a doubt, was sincere in his claim that it did. He witnessed the native silhouetted woman that night, wild and free. I saw it in his eyes. He was oblivious to the reality that he also was out speeding through the desert to escape, to grasp an elusive freedom from everything that was encumbering his life. The parallel was so obvious to me.

I said nothing. I thought about sailors of olden

days and the myth of mermaids. It's been said the origin of the mermaid legend was rooted in their longing to combine a desired image—a woman, absent from their seafaring existence—with their ocean surroundings.

Did it happen? Werner was a man who lived for the extraordinary and the extemporaneous. From the beginning, I knew he was scheduled to live in New York for two years only, and then he would return to Germany. He had told me so. But we were having such an exuberant time that the fact it would be ending was not considered. Our life together had a wanderlust, a stardust, so much that its sudden halt was unimaginable.

But our days were diminishing, before we realized it. Werner's stay in the States would be ending in about three more months. I treasured every aspect of our relationship. The friendship ... the romance ... the sensuality ... the adventure ... the sheer fun.

Then it came. The question from him. "How would you feel about going back to Germany with me?"

I blinked. I was startled yet somewhat honored. I shrugged. "It never crossed my mind."

This was not the answer he wanted. How could I answer him just like that? But to me, his calm, sincere, meaningful question felt like an ambush on my mind and emotions. From that moment on, I was beset with thoughts only about this proposal. Could I just pack up and leave? To relocate my entire life, not to another city but to another country?

To be honest, there was a lot I did miss about Germany. I love history, and Germany had plenty of it. Starting with numerous castles hundreds of years old. Tudor-style houses older than the existing United States. The breathtaking landscapes, the rugged mountains, the green valleys, all of this I missed dearly. And there was a sentimental remnant in my heart toward the country where I was born, where I grew up. Still, the United States was the country I had chosen. That's of paramount importance when staring at a life-changing decision.

Pondering his question, I kept thinking of so much here that I'd miss as well, maybe more. I had build up a comfortable life here in the States: a great job in a travel agency, my own house, and most of all, freedom—feeling free, something I never had in Germany. Memories of my childhood entered my mind, me being trapped in a place I hated with passion. Returning to live there again would only stir up memories I liked to forget.

Because I chose America to be the home where I could live my adult life, a bond was sealed. Was my bond with Werner strong enough to conquer it—to change not only my mind but my lifestyle, my friends, my job, my neighborhood, my community, my entire future?

The problem was I did not know, at least this moment; all I knew was that I was not going to get any younger. I was in my early forties, at an age when things in life are starting to change, more drastically than when I was in my twenties or thirties, and chances of meeting someone would be harder with each passing year. Did I love him? Was I in love with him?

As much as I really wanted to be with him, I felt just as strongly that I was not ready for such a dramatic, life-changing commitment. During the critical weeks that followed, my mind and heart were fighting their own tug-of-war. The chances of meeting someone or being with someone were still good, but what about in another five to ten years? As I was getting older, I felt the years pass so much faster. I was leaning toward the idea of being with Werner, but I also was leaning toward the idea of staying here, a place that had become my second home and represented freedom.

What was the right thing to do? I asked myself many times over. Relentlessly, I steeped my soul deep into questions that only I could answer. I knew whatever decision I made, I would either regret it for the rest of my life or be satisfied that it was the right choice. The problem was I did not know.

What if I went back to Germany with him? I'd have to start all over again, pursue a new job, new friends, deal with a new place to live. Meanwhile, I'd be completely dependent on Werner. It would be unavoidable! As an electrical engineer, Werner, of course, had a job waiting for him in Germany, but I, on the other hand, would have to start looking for something new again. I'd have to rely on him for so much—socially, emotionally, financially—at least in the beginning.

What if it didn't work out the way I wanted, the way he wanted? How did I want it to work out anyway? What if, after time passed, it all fell apart? Or I lost interest? Or he lost interest? Stuck! I'd be stuck!

In hindsight, I see there was nothing to support my racing anxieties about my biggest concern—loss of interest in each other. Knowing him as intimately as I did over our two years together, the fact was he was not a fickle man. He was, after all, ten years my senior, and he believed I would be happy with him. Looking back with wisdom from the perspective of time, where I am now, I admit it was all about my fear. I was afraid I would be without a quick escape plan if and when I might wake up one morning with a change of heart. I thought of many times in my life I had exhibited my chameleon ways. In my years, I was always very impulsive, made decisions without thinking them through, which most of the time got me in situations. This time, I promised myself, it would not happen again. I could not afford to keep making the same mistakes I made when I was younger. Often, commitments were made on impulse, only to realize soon after it was a mistake.

And two years together was not sufficient evidence to me that my fear of losing my freedom and precious autonomy would disappear. The question had ignited enormous conflict inside of me: But we have so much fun together! He's exciting! I like him! No, I love him! Don't I?

After endless self-examination and life inventory, my final answer was no. I had too many ties to my life in America, my own home, my own friends and work. I did not see myself ever feeling comfortable in a version of his life. Depending on him while managing my reentry into Germany-as-home again would overwhelm me. I wasn't able to predict that our living together in Germany would be a success. And the truth is he did not offer a proposal of marriage for a reason. He had been burned—no, scorched—from years in a distressed marriage, one that ultimately melded into an acidic divorce.

Would it have made a difference if he asked me to marry him? Maybe but probably not. I had been divorced at a young age, and freedom was my first priority since getting out of that mistake. So my final answer was no. And I insisted that we break all ties.

We made plans to meet at our favorite place, the Duck Pond Inn in Bay Shore.

"Yes, Vicky, six o'clock at the Duck Pond Inn should be good."

After hanging up the phone, I was trying to think how to give Werner the news. All I knew was that over the years I had become experienced enough to recognize what I was looking for before making any important decisions, especially when it came to relationships.

Six o'clock sharp, I showed up at the Duck Pond Inn and saw Werner's car already in the parking lot. I knew he must be waiting anxiously. As I entered the restaurant, I saw Werner sitting at the bar waiting for me.

"Have you been waiting long?" I asked him.

"Maybe twenty minutes," he answered.

"Is it possible we can take a table with a little more privacy?"

"Sure, Vicky. What about the one over there in the corner?"

"Perfect. Let's go!" I ordered a drink before we both headed for the table.

"What is the occasion for our meeting?"

"Let me come to the point, Werner. I feel like it would be best talking to you face-to-face regarding the question you asked me not too long ago—how I would feel about returning to Germany with you."

"How can I forget a question so important to me?"

"Werner, I have thought about your question long and hard, including the plus and minuses, and at the end, I came to the conclusion not to return with you to Germany."

Werner looked at me with a very surprised look; I guess this was not the answer he expected.

"Believe me, Werner, it was not an easy decision. I thought about it endlessly, and in the end, I decided against it, not because I did not enjoy the time with you and the places we went. I will always cherish the time I had with you."

"Vicky!" It was all I could hear despite the din in the bar. Then, of course, the question. "Why? I thought we had something special going. These two years together gave me a feeling of being wanted again. The times we shared were wonderful and unforgettable."

"Werner, please see my point of view. I do care for you, so much. We had two wonderful years together, and I will cherish the time we had together for the rest of my life. I have been thinking of the whole situation, and believe me, it was not an easy decision."

"Look at me, Vicky." Werner gently took my face into his hands. "Tell me that you will think it over again. Then let me know what your answer will be."

But my mind was made up. It was my firm decision. And I refused to maintain a long-distance friendship with him. What good would that do? I honestly believed a clean break was the best decision, the way to go. I had learned over the years not to hold on to something that only would lead me to nowhere, or to a relationship with uncertainty.

Today, the story is different. I never forgot him. I think about him still. I think of our time together. Often I have asked myself if I should have gone with him. I have asked myself, did I make a terrible mistake? Each time I ask, I valiantly answer that I have no regrets. But sometimes I wonder.

Chapter 7

THE ROAD TO HELL IS PAVED WITH ANTI-AGING CREAM

SOMETHING HAD TO change. In the late 1980s, I was in my mid-forties, and the feeling of getting old fast was stuck in my mind. There was no way possible to turn back the chronological clock. I had to do something to recover the years I had lost and felt I was still entitled to enjoy.

How good do we have to look anyway? How could I (or any woman "of a certain age") feel good about myself while television, movies, tabloids, pop culture, and even my own girlfriends were verifying that menopausal women are sex-appeal-free?

One morning in 1989, I was getting dressed for the day. It was a warm day in late spring, and

I decided to wear a sleeveless blouse. Checking myself in the mirror before I left the house, I noticed another development that horrified me— the gradual emergence of "bat-wings"—those fleshy folds that develop in middle age—hanging from my arms! No! I was wearing a short-sleeve blouse on a sultry summer day.

Studying myself in the mirror, I realized my muscles were starting to go. My knees were growing wrinkly and baggy too. Even they were not exempt from this aging demon. My immediate solution was to stop wearing short sleeves and pants above my knees. But that was only a cover-up, not a real solution to the problem.

In hindsight, I should have put a halt to this self-scrutiny. I should have asked myself, "Victoria, don't you have better things to do than stare at yourself in the mirror?" But no, I didn't stop myself. Rather, I allowed myself to be hypnotized by my own reflection. My fading physical beauty was becoming my number-one concern. In fact, it grew into a perverse kind of self-pity.

Inexplicably, I actually welcomed mourning! That's what I was doing, after all—mourning the progressive erosion of my youthful good looks.

Snap out of this wallowing! I told myself. I tried to rally against my unhappy self-image, which was firmly centered on my physical appearance. To love myself just the way I was—what a nice idea! But at that time, I was having none of it. What I wanted desperately was to turn back the clock.

Later that month, I decided to call my friend Brit. That day, I asked her, "Brit, how would you feel if we spent a day just clothes shopping?" I wanted to keep my mind busy, other than thinking about what else I could do to turn back that clock.

"Vicky, that's a great idea! I haven't done any clothes shopping in a while. It's time. I'm running out of what else I can wear."

"Great! What about this weekend? How do Macy's, Saks Fifth Avenue, Bloomingdales, and Lord and Taylor sound to you?"

"Sounds great! Let's go for it!" So we made our plans.

Shopping for clothes always gave me a little lift emotionally, even if only temporarily. But on this day, I wasn't lifted up but beaten down. When Brit and I met that weekend, I dressed in comfortable shoes, as I knew we had a lot of walking to get done. I was glad she decided to come with me so she could give me input about what looked good on me. I trusted her judgment on clothing.

Our first stop was Macy's. We took the elevator to the fifth floor, which was the department for women. There was just so much to look at. It felt overwhelming. I aimed for a rack not far from us. I had a special look in mind; it had to be light in color, sporty, and sophisticated. Then I saw a pretty outfit on one of the mannequins and asked the salesperson where I could find that kind of outfit.

She told us to follow her and went in the opposite direction. "Here's where you will find it," she said with a smile.

Brit and I got busy going through the rack, looking for the outfit that the mannequin was wearing. "Lets try it on," I said to Brit and started walking toward the changing room. How I loved to go clothes shopping even if I had to keep changing into a new outfit many times over. It was not always fun, but it came with the territory. I checked myself in the mirror. Yes, it was a nice outfit, but somehow it did not look as nice on me as it had on the mannequin.

I stepped out of the changing room to get Brit's opinion. "What do you think of this, Brit?"

She looked at me. "I like the outfit, but for some reason it looks so much different on you."

"You know, Brit, I was thinking the same thing."

"I guess just because it looks nice on the mannequin does not always mean it will look nice on anyone else. So this one is out!" We decided to look some more.

I hadn't realized that Brit was gone, and then I heard Brit asking me, "What do you think about this outfit, Vicky?"

She'd decided to try on the same outfit I was just wearing.

"It looks nice, Brit, and for some reason it looks so much better on you than it does on me." This felt a bit discouraging, but I tried to rally. "Why don't we look at other department stores? We can always come back here if we do not find anything else."

"Yes, let's not make a quick decision till we see what other stores have. We may find something else better and cheaper."

We left Macy's, heading for Bloomingdales down the road. Arriving at the Bloomingdales department store, we aimed for the women's clothing area. There was just so much to look at. It certainly was not easy finding something to our liking, but we had the whole day set aside, so we took all the time we needed to find that perfect outfit. We both were busy trying on different outfits and did not notice how time went by. We finally decided on a few nice tops and bottoms, realizing it was getting late and time to head home. We both agreed to find a place to sit down for a cup of coffee or tea. Living in New York, you have no problem finding a nice place to relax to end the day. We were both exhausted, but I'd bought some new clothes and had that little rush of fun doing it.

***

Some months later, after that shopping trip, the seemingly inevitable choice of seriously looking into having something done about my face loomed in and out of my thoughts. I felt it was time for more serious changes to improve my looks, other than a nice youthful haircut and a new youthful wardrobe. Each time I looked into the mirror, it seemed like there was a new wrinkle or gray hair.

Cosmetic surgery? Was this the solution? Could it transform me? Could it transform me? Would it make me look how I wanted to look again? Would it render the revitalized version of myself I was longing for? Was I crazy to consider it? On the other hand, what did I have to lose? I reasoned. It was worth a try. Or so I thought.

My decision was made: I was going to see a plastic surgeon. I picked up the phone to call Brit again. She'd had some work done (as they say) about three years before we met. As best friends now, we confided in each other about almost everything.

"Victoria? What's up?"

In an almost hushed voice, I confided, "It's time, Brit. I looked in the mirror one time too many, and I'm seeing things I don't want to see, if you know what I mean."

"Oh my god! Are you saying what I think you're saying?"

"Yes! Give me his number. Brit, I am not ready to deal with what we call aging, the lines in my face, looseness of my skin, a gray here and there. It's time for me to do something about it. No matter what it takes, I am determined!"

And so she did, with some cheerleader encouragement. "He's really very good, Victoria. I was happy with my results. You won't regret it."

"If he does as good of a job on me like he did on you, I will be more than happy." We continued some small talk, but anxious, I didn't want to wait any longer.

My next step was to rouse the courage to make the appointment. Seems he really was the local cosmetic surgeon of choice, because his schedule was booked solid for weeks. After looking through the appointment book, the receptionist finally found an opening for me to come in for a consultation. The day of the appointment, I was pretty nervous. What kind of treatment would he suggest? Filler, laser, or perhaps a facelift?

The waiting room was furnished with exclusive and tasteful furniture and couch-like chairs, almost like a living room setting, most definitely for patients to feel at ease.

Wow, did I have the jitters! Discreetly, I surveyed the several women and the lone man already seated in the waiting room. Their presence had both a positive and negative influence on me. *First*, I told myself, *I'm not alone. See—look at these other people who want change in their lives.* All of us sitting there shared an unspoken solidarity. *What are they feeling?* I wondered. That's when I realized they were not satisfied with themselves. Were they in mourning like me? Because that's a terrible way to be! A sinking feeling took over my stomach.

After a wait of about forty minutes, the receptionist called my name. "Please come in, Ms. Janosevic. The doctor is waiting. You can take a seat," she instructed when I finally entered this in-demand doctor's office. The room was well lit. On the wall hung his diplomas; there were several of them, very impressive. Seated behind a huge desk was the doctor, in his sixties, with gray hair and looking very distinguished. As I entered the room, he got up and greeted me with a firm handshake.

"Please sit down, Ms. Janosevic!"

I sat gratefully, still a bit nervous.

"What can I do for you, Ms. Janosevic? Why are you here?" He was amiable, professional, and obviously quite experienced at putting patients at ease.

"I want to look more like myself again,

Doctor. Myself, that is, before these lines and creases began showing up."

He explained several procedures—laser, fillers, and facelift surgery—and I am telling you that some of them sounded a little terrifying. You hear stories of surgeries not being successful, with different outcomes and not so happy endings. But I wanted to do this! I wanted change. I wanted to feel good again whenever I looked in the mirror. We talked for a while. He discussed various options to determine that the best procedure for me would be fillers, a substance that is injected into the lines of the face to puff it up a little to make any line less noticeable.

The mutual understanding we reached was that surgery was not necessary yet. "Let's start with a few filler injections. It's minimally invasive, and you'll see a difference soon."

I did not want to wait much longer or make another appointment, so I decided to start right away while I was in the office. He suggested starting with a filler, which is not the same as Botox. Filler is a fluid that gets injected into the lines to puff it up a little to make the wrinkle less noticeable.

Ten minutes … that felt like ten weeks. I am not a fan of needles, especially when they're being inserted into my face! I forced myself to endure. And I did. I pulled through because I wanted this so badly. Then he handed me the dreaded mirror. Amazing! It worked! I absolutely looked years younger. The lines were gone, and the cheeks looked more puffy and youthful! I vowed this was the beginning of a good, new relationship with the mirror. Filler injections seemed to do a great job.

Delighted with this first treatment, I walked into that building a middle-aged woman and walked out a girl—a girl who had just been awarded another shot at lost time.

"There will be some redness, but it will disappear in a few days," he told me. Apparently the good doctor was also a master of the understatement. I needed another fix, but a serious gaze in the mirror back home, and I had to smile, in spite of myself. My face looked like a proverbial pincushion! Some redness, indeed! My face had the extra-added "attraction" of being swollen for days afterward. Like a boxer who just heard, "You're out!" hollered by the referee.

"Oh, it's an allergic reaction from a new facial cleanser I tried," I lied when people asked, but that was my story, and I was sticking to it whenever anybody asked. But guess what? The final result came abut three days later, and I looked beautiful! There was light swelling at the beginning, but now this was gone as well and made the whole face even more youthful. Floating on puffy pink clouds of recovered self-esteem, I marveled again at this small procedure that made it happen. And how richly I deserved it. Disappointments will always be a part of life, and the risk of becoming bitter can certainly accompany them. I must admit the decision of having filler done and the result did not bring any disappointments.

But, of course, time kept marching on, and I did too—again and again, I marched into Doctor Feel-Good's Youth Emporium. I kept an appointment with him about every eight to ten months. I knew that the body builds up a resistance toward foreign objects, and the filler substance was no different. I didn't want to wait too long so that lines in my face would start showing again due to resistance.

How long would this hold on? How long could

I keep this up? It's not authentic, and why was I doing this to myself? An uneasiness crept in, and in the end, approximately six to eight years after my first injection, the Youth Emporium failed me. Eventually my face looked like a construction site with all the needle punctures. My anti-aging campaign ended in failure.

Or did it? So many of us would like to be perfect. But why? Behind each imperfection lurks the fear of it, of not measuring up to some standard. I thought I was staying a few steps ahead of time, and oh, how dynamic I was. But it became a burdensome drain on me, sucking my zest for life as I was clinging to the past. That was it; I wasn't living my life, not really. The past was too important to me. And although it might never be completely erased from my soul, I needed to accept the past for what it was: over.

This is how I escaped! The trap of mourning lost youth and the fear of not being perfect—I left them behind as I switched my destination. I had to find another way to return to that youthful look. I stepped off of that road to hell and started living in the moment.

Chapter 8

DO IT YOURSELF

Do it yourself—a common refrain for many folks, including those looking to preserve their looks. I knew there had to be another way to get that youthful look, perhaps cheaper than a plastic surgeon, and I was going to find one. Paying each visit for one injection had a price tag of about $500 to $800, which could add up quite a bit, depending how many injections were necessary to cover each wrinkle. My own experience was that fillers were not a forever solution unless you were willing to keep paying a high price for it. I knew that I could not stop the aging process, but this should not stop me from trying either; I was determined to find a way. I wanted something more lasting than the fillers but with just about as much as of an impact in appearance.

For the next couple of days, I had nothing else on my mind but to find that answer. One evening I was sitting in my living room with a *Glamour* magazine in my hand, and I started to look through the pages. It was one of the magazines showing photos of celebrities all made up. Women like Madonna, Kate Moss, Debra Messing, Courtney Cox. These were actors and models you would never recognize without makeup; they are just like average people. However, we seem so blinded by their perfections and become so obsessed with wanting to look like them that we are willing to pay any price.

As I turned the pages, I was a little puzzled. It showed famous celebrities before and after their makeovers. It was hard to believe what a difference clothes and a little makeup could make; most of them I would never have recognized without that makeover. In fact, the photos of model Naomi Campbell, before she was wearing makeup and then after, with makeup, surprised me the most; I was literally speechless. I would have *never* guessed that it was the same person. That was when I saw the power of a makeover. Those pictures went through my head over and over. It just proved to me what a little makeup and wearing some nice clothes could do to a person. It most definitely did not have the same price tag as one filler with a cosmetic surgeon.

Then I realized this was the answer I was looking for! I was going to change my appearance not through a cosmetic surgeon this time but by "do it yourself," without a big price tag attached to office visits. I knew I had to make some changes, and I felt this was an answer. I was tired of spending time and money, worrying so much about aging, knowing the fact that worry is one of the biggest problems facing mankind. Unfortunately, we go into maturity with little preparation for what lies ahead. With all the modern technology we have today, no one has yet found eternal youth.

There was nothing I could do but make the best out of the situation and let nothing stop me. To me, life is like a journey where we have to start somewhere, and I decided to start within myself. If I could not find that inner peace with myself, I would never find it anywhere else.

***

One day at the travel agency, my coworker Linda gave me something to look at. We'd been working together in a travel agency for about three years. I had to be in my early forties, a time when changes within you seem to appear.

"Wait a minute," I said. "I have to get my glasses." I'd been using them since my eyes got weaker.

Linda looked at me intently. "Vicky, wow, I cannot believe how smart you look with those glasses on. You should wear them more often. Go check yourself in the mirror!"

I went into the bathroom mirror to check out what she was talking about, and to my surprise, she was right! I also noticed that because of the reflection of the glass, the little lines around my eyes were barley noticeable. What a nice surprise! Soon after that, I went out and bought myself several pairs of glasses in different colors with the thought that each outfit could have a matching color. The glasses were not prescription glasses but were meant to make a fashion statement, and they most certainly did. Wearing glasses became almost essential to me.

My next step was going clothes shopping again.

I was aiming for a particular style, refreshing in looks. I was eager to start the change. This gave me a natural high, a feeling we all know very well from our childhood, always anxious for something new and different. In the next couple of days, I was busy thinking of all the other changes I was going to implement, as changes with my living space were also on the horizon. I wanted to start one thing first before continuing to the next.

For one, I knew I wanted to buy a different wardrobe, a more youthful one, most important lighter in color—whites, creams, pale yellows, greens, royal blues, and even some reds—sporty and yet sophisticated. I never paid much attention to color till I noticed one day that dark colors made me look worn out. What we buy tells us who we want to be, and I wanted to give the image of appearing younger and most of all more youthful. I knew this would also reflect on the way I was feeling about myself.

I knew I was going in the right direction. For the next days and weeks, I got caught up in the excitement. It was a wonderful feeling. Many women like to go shopping anyway and don't need to have a reason. I felt like I was turning over a new leaf. Department stores like Macy's, Bloomingdales, Lord and Taylor, and Saks Fifth Avenue were my favorites, and when I shopped, they seemed to have everything to my liking. I spent the next days planning on the kind of clothing I was going to buy. A weekend was coming up. I had no big plans, and my friend Brit had a family get-together, so I decided to go clothes shopping by myself.

I aimed for my favored department stores, the ones I knew had exactly what I was looking for. I must have been in my own world of excitement, on a natural high, when I heard a voice behind me say, "Can I help you? What are you looking for? Perhaps I can be of some assistance?" A sales clerk peered at me hopefully.

"Oh that is nice of you. I am looking for clothes more toward sporty and yet sophisticated." She pointed in a direction to let me know where to find it.

I politely thanked her and went back into my shopping mode. I concentrated on light and cheery colors. It was not an easy task to find something to my liking; there were just so many different varieties of clothing. However, before deciding on a particular item, I was going to see what else I could find at other stores. After several hours of running from one store to another, I finally found a few things to my liking. "This will do for a start," I told myself.

I could not wait to get home and try on my new outfits, as that was something I enjoyed a lot. When I got home, my first thought was to try on the new outfits I bought that day. After unwinding first from a busy day, I was ready for another private fashion show of my own. With great excitement, I took my new treasure of clothing out of my shopping bag. One by one, I tried them on and looked at myself in the mirror. I was very pleased with what I saw. Thanks to my slim figure, all the new outfits looked so great. "I love it," I whispered to myself.

But wait; there was something else. I tried to figure it out, what it could be. "It's not the new outfit; it fits great in every way." From the neck down, I looked great. Then what else could it be? Yes, this was it! At the time, I was wearing my hair a little more than shoulder length. When I was in my teens into my twenties, I looked great with long hair. However, as we age, even the hair texture changes, and long hair can make a woman look drawn. I held my hair back to get an idea of what it might look like shorter. To my surprise, it made a huge difference.

The next day, I called up a hair salon to make an appointment and was lucky to get an opening. As I was waiting for my turn, I looked at magazines with different hairstyles. There were so many it was hard to pick one. Then it was my turn.

"What can I do for you today?" was the girl's question.

"I checked out your magazines. There were a few nice haircuts, which makes it hard to decide."

We both had a look at the magazine.

"Well, what do you suggest?" I asked her, showing her three different styles. We both looked at it for a moment, and she then pointed to one photo. "I think this would make you look great and so much younger." Looking younger was my goal.

"Okay, let's go for it!" I said.

About thirty minutes later, she was done. As I looked in the mirror, I was speechless. I would have never thought what a difference a nice haircut would make.

"Why didn't I thought about this earlier?" I said to the girl. I got up to pay and left a nice tip since she did such a great job.

With a new haircut and a new wardrobe, I felt like a new woman and sure looked like one. I could not wait to show Brit my new outfits and haircut and see her reaction. That same evening, I called Brit to talk about my day. "Let me tell you about my weekend. I took advantage of a weekend with no plans to do some clothes shopping."

"That sounds great. How was it?"

"Well I don't have to tell you, but I was in my glory! I'm anxious to tell you all about it."

We made plans to meet that Friday at a cute little place in Bay Shore called Duck Pond Inn. It was cute little restaurant with a bar where you could see a lake through a wall-to-wall window, a cozy and relaxing atmosphere.

I was looking forward to meeting Brit, and when Friday came, I got ready wearing some of my new clothes. I decided to wear a pair of white jeans, a white top, red, ankle, high-heel boots, a red purse, a red tailored leather jacket, and of course my new red glasses. I glanced in the mirror.

I must admit I was impressed! I could not wait to hear what Brit had to say.

We met Friday as planned at our favored little place. As I entered the bar, I saw Brit already waiting for me, her back toward the entrance door. I walked over and tapped her on her shoulder. "Hi, Brit!"

Brit turned around, facing me. "Vicky, is this really you? Oh my God, you look great! I would have never guessed that clothes, a new haircut, and glasses could change a person so much! I have no words—and look at those glasses! They make you look so smart! This makes me think that I may need a change like this myself." Her eyes were wide, and she wore an excited smile. She reached out and touched the leather jacket. "I love this! Where did you buy it? I cannot believe how soft this feels. It feels like butter."

"Yes, I loved it the moment I laid eyes on it. It was at Saks Fifth Avenue. I had to get it. It was love at first sight."

I had accomplished my mission! I ordered my favorite drink, Baileys on the rocks, and pulled over one of the bar-stools next to her. "Brit, tell me all about your weekend!"

As we got involved in a conversation, I felt someone tapping on my shoulder. I turned around to see who it was. I saw a young man at least thirty years my junior.

"I don't want to be impolite, interrupting your conversation," he said.

"Oh no, don't worry. You're not interrupting," I responded with a smile.

"I have been watching you for a while," the young man continued. "I hope you don't mind me saying it, but I love your glasses. They look very sexy."

I was speechless. Was he really talking to me? I did not give a response I was so surprised. I had never gotten such a wonderful compliment, even after I had fillers for my face.

Right then I knew I did the right thing, bringing change not only to my face but to my entire self.

After that, I started to feel so much better. The fillers, the clothes, the haircut, and the glasses lifted my self-esteem quite a bit. From all the compliments I got, I knew it was the best thing I had done in a while. I knew I had gone in the right direction.

Then one day I looked around my house and decided to change the place where I spend so much of my time. After all, this was a place where I spent the majority of my life. I saw it first thing in the morning when I woke up until the evening when I went to sleep. A home is like the outer skin of our soul, which affects and influences our mood and mirrors our character, a place where we can leave the world outside. A home is like a refuge, a place I find serenity.

Not much later, I called Ben, a handyman that friends had often used to fix things around the house. Everybody liked his work and was very happy with him. I asked him to paint the inside of my house. At the time, the walls were all white, in my eyes a way too sterile color, so I decided on pale green for the walls and a touch of darker green for the doors and moldings.

A few days later when he was finished, I could hardly believe it; everything looked so nice and cheery. It was most certainly a welcome change. Everyone who came into my house loved it. It was like I was moving into a brand-new place, with a brand-new me. All around, I felt great.

The battle, it seemed, was over.

Chapter 9

LEARNING TO FLY

AT THE AGE of forty-two, after revamping my wardrobe and my home, I still wanted something to look forward to. Something was still missing in my life. I had just stepped off the road to hell and left behind my obsession with having a youthful appearance. No more cosmetic injections. No more trips to the plastic surgeon. No more hours in front of the mirror worrying about something I couldn't stop anyway.

But now what? At that time, longevity was not an issue to me. I was still young enough, in my early forties, to keep fighting, strong enough for the next round in my world championship match: me versus aging.

So I started to ask myself: What do I want? What will bring me joy and happiness in my daily life? What is missing now?

I knew I should start counting my blessings instead the lines on my face, (which I'd made myself stop inspecting on a daily basis). All together I had a comfortable life: a nice job in a travel agency that allowed me to do what I like most—traveling. I had a lovely home that I'd just redecorated. I had friends to spend time with.

I needed to be looking outside of myself instead at myself in the mirror. To pay attention to the things I had and stop mourning what I didn't have.

These deliberate efforts to be constructive were a first step to somewhere ... a cliché but still true: life is a journey. Now that I extracted myself from the road to hell, I had to resume this journey to somewhere. And if I couldn't establish some kind of peace within, I would still be on a road to nowhere.

The next step: I collected some peppy, cheer-myself-on affirmations. Here are the ones that helped me the most:

Get dressed and show up. Always try to do

your best. Don't fall apart just because everything isn't going your way. Look for beauty in life and appreciate it. Choose to be confident. Relax and go with the flow. Allow good things to come your way. Be grateful for your health. Refuse to worry!

Yesterday and tomorrow—I had to let them go and stop worrying about them! Actually, some of these corny motivational statements took root. They became kernels of hope, I think, somewhere in my soul. I began to feel a direction taking form, a sense of control finding its way back to me. I would no longer be a compulsory victim of time. "Time marches on." "Time waits for no one." I had heard these clichés too often and had to make these sentiments work for me, not against me. I was not, after all, a victim of time.

And if time waits for no one, well, how does that sentiment apply to me? It has to do with living in the moment, I reasoned. But how do I do that? My questions kept coming at me ... Do I have undiscovered talents I never knew about before? Was I guilty of underestimating myself all these years?

Deep down, all I wanted was to be happy. Doesn't everybody? To be whatever I want to be (like happy), I reasoned, has everything to do with how I live my life every single day.

To live happier … to live happier. That was it! There I was, in the middle of my life, with each moment coming and going. Time. I needed to catch those moments and live inside each one of them. Live in the moment. I could do that! Isn't that how children live? In the moment? To do this, there always needs to be something new to look forward to, something that is available and on the way. I was determined to believe that something good was going to happen, something I never did before.

That was it! Every day, I needed to expect something new and good to happen. I knew one thing for sure: whatever it was, it was going to be for me and me only.

It was one of those almost spring days in March 1991, the kind that's not quite warm enough to stay outside very long, even though you're dying to after a never-ending winter.

On that particular day, I was tooling along in my shiny little black Volkswagen. I happened to glance over at the Farmingdale airport, a small airport on Long Island, New York. As I drove past its expanse, a Technicolor image flashed in my mind. Me, Victoria, a trained, skilled, and licensed pilot! Me, Victoria, triumphant and accomplished! I could feel the excitement and wonder about my dream bubbling in my chest as I drove by the airport.

I could not wait to tell my friend Brit all about my idea. What would she say? That evening, I called Brit, and we made plans to meet on Friday at Pier 44, a small restaurant by the bay. After hanging up the phone, the thought of learning how to fly did not leave my mind. I could not wait till Friday to tell Brit all about it; I wanted to talk to her in person and see her face and her reaction,

After we met at the restaurant, she looked me over. "I am anxious about what news you have to tell me that you would not tell me over the phone.

"Baileys on the rocks, please," I said to the bartender. I turned back to her and took a deep breath. "Okay, are you ready for this?"

"Yes, of course, Vicky. Shoot."

"What do you think of me learning how to fly?"

"Wow!" A pause. "But why?"

"Why not?" I replied. "Look, I know I'm not twenty years old, but is there an expiration date for a woman to learn something new? Not only that, I also want to prove a point here, that women are certainly capable of handling machines larger and more powerful than cars. What about Amelia Earhart? You know lots of people, including you American baby boomers. I think if Earhart had lived, things would be different now. She would have used her celebrity to open doors, doors of opportunity for women to crash the boys' club of the commercial airline industry. And think about it. When you board a plane, can you come up with one legitimate reason why you almost never see a female pilot at the cockpit door?" (Only about 7 percent of commercial pilots are female.)

Studying Brit's face for a reaction, I could see she was impressed. "I wish I had your courage," she sighed.

"Wait and see. I will fly as good as any male pilot and better than some."

Yet even as I spoke those words, the truth was I had to prove it to myself too. But I wasn't going to admit this to anyone. My decision was made.

My "something new" was for me only. Something good was about to happen to me. I was nervous.

***

My first flying lesson took place on a sunny day in September 1991, in Brookhaven, New York, at a small private airport with very little air traffic, perfect for starting as a new student pilot. There were no qualifying tests to enroll in flight school because testing would come later.

My flight instructor, Dave, was the embodiment of professionalism: friendly, displaying a comfortable balance of skill and self-confidence. He was fit, and the word "medium" was an apt choice to describe his physical appearance. Medium height, medium weight, medium brown hair cropped so short it made him look like a somewhat overage West Point cadet.

That first orientation day was all about getting the feel of being in the pilot's seat. Dave was familiarizing me with the instruments, what each one was for and how to use them. The yoke is the same as a steering wheel in a car. We talked about the use of a rudder. Rudder is for the primary purpose to prevent yaw. Yaw is the rotation of the airplane about its vertical axis, which often and appropriately is called the yaw axis. And so on. Dave oriented us to many concepts of flight and flying a small plane.

Dave also taught me about the preflight and what needed to be done, because the preflight preparation is very important. He gave me a list with all the preflight preparations. No matter of how good of a pilot you are, it must be done every single time. Even a commercial pilot with many hours of fly time is not exempt.

Dave went with me through the list and showed me what needed to be done. Walk around the plane, check for any damages on the wing or propeller, and check the fuel tank to make sure it's full with gas. We had to know the weight and balance, which is very important, as it tells you how much a plane can carry in order to keep the right balance. Then it was time to do a check of all the instruments and make sure all was in working order. Everything seemed fine, so we were ready to start our lesson.

All I really did that first day of class was hold the yoke, the apparatus equivalent to the steering wheel in a car. It was enough for me to know what to expect. It was good, though, a really good feeling, one that felt like a bit of mastery and power. Most of the flight training was in the plane itself, one-to-one with my instructor.

The other part of training consisted of group classroom sessions to prepare us for the test we would eventually be taking in order to be licensed. Of the twenty students in my class, I was the only woman. Determined, yes. Nervous, yes. Both. But not worried because deep down I really knew I could do this. This would work because I would make it work.

A flight student's progress is measured by the number of hours in the air flying with the instructor. Seventy is the average number of hours to log before taking the big step to the first solo flight. It's really about your comfort level. Some students preferred to take more than seventy hours. The most important skills required are mastering a successful takeoff and landing. Radio operation and communicating with the airport tower are also essential and of utmost importance.

Each airport has its own unique signature radio frequency, which is important because it is the only communication you have while in the air. I had to master these. You cannot take off without the okay from the tower first. The way to identify yourself is through a number on the plane, which can be read on the tail of each small plane. Since I was still in training, I flew several different training planes, all having their own ID numbers.

With each lesson, I just got better and better. Being so high off the ground and looking down from the plane felt like an adventure itself. To be sure the plane was leveled, my flight instructor pointed out a spot on the horizon. "Keep it in sight and you know that your plane is leveled," Dave said. Each little instrument had a different meaning. At first it felt impossible to remember, but with time, I even had this in full control. Being so high up off the ground, all you see is the sky around you; it feels like you are on top of the world, certainly a nice feeling.

Soon after, my flight instructor sent me for a written test on April 29, 1992. On arrival, I was presented with a list of one hundred questions and was told a score of sixty-five was the minimum to pass this test. Then the instructor left the room. I was all by myself. About one hour later, I felt

I was done and hoped to have enough points to pass the written exam. I got up and left the room.

Outside, I was met by my exam instructor. I gave him my papers. I was told I would receive the result in about four weeks. I must say these were the tensest weeks. After four weeks of intense waiting, I finally received my result. As I held the envelope in my hands, I was wondering what it could say. Then I opened the envelope, and to my surprise, I passed my written test with flying colors. Out of a hundred questions, I had only two wrong, which gave me a ninety-six!

After completing the written test, I also had to perform a couple of landings and takeoffs without any help from Dave.

At my first takeoff, Dave was sitting in the copilot seat, but he didn't say a word. As I navigated that impressively powerful machine up into the air, a fortune-cookie proverb seared though my brain: "If you let go, you will have both hands free." No, I didn't let go of the yoke! But I am telling you, old baggage hidden far down in my soul for years was lifting. I let go! And I was as light as the air I was flying my plane through. Both of my hands were freed from clutching memories I didn't even know had been keeping me in shackles.

Memories from my childhood prisons. Memories from a failed marriage. Memories of my flying dreams and being thwarted by high walls. But overwhelmingly, this moment in the air was a personal triumph over the memories of a lifetime, and I finally realized the significance of my childhood prisons' connection to my dread and fear of aging.

But on this day in May 1992, I was prepping for my first solo landing without my instructor, Dave's, help. We were flying out of the Brookhaven airport, which was located about sixty miles east of NYC. It was a small private airport, perfect for a first solo takeoff and landing.

After practicing a few takeoffs and landings, Dave turned to me. "Victoria, you did great on those landings and takeoffs, but now it's your turn to do it without me as a copilot." Dave told me to maneuver the plane off the runway.

My stomach dropped a bit in my belly. "What are you talking about?"

"What I mean is I feel you are good enough

to do your fist solo takeoff and landings on your own. I will sign off on this."

Signing a student pilot off for a first solo was a must; no solo without a signoff. "David, are you sure I am ready?"

"Of course you are. Do you really think I would take a chance having any of my students do a solo if I thought they were not ready? I could lose my license as a flight instructor."

"Okay, if you say so. I trust you on this."

Dave climbed down from the cockpit. All alone, I sat there trying to get my thoughts together on what to do next. I was too nervous to think straight. Then I remembered and dialed in the frequency of the Farmingdale airport. "November 7577 Lima," I said. "Requesting takeoff."

I waited a moment for a response. Then I heard a voice from the tower. "Lima 7577, clear for takeoff."

My heart must have been beating a hundred miles an hour. I kept telling myself, "Relax, Vicky. If Dave thinks I am ready, then yes, I am ready."

I slowly pushed the throttle to rev the engine's speed of my Cessna 152, waited to reach takeoff speed, and then slowly pulled the yoke (steering wheel) of the plane toward me. The plane started to lift. I climbed up to the recommended speed then prepared for a turn back to the airport to do the three required takeoffs and landings, which were needed for a successful solo flight. Doing turns, I was not yet too confident about it, but I had no choice. All the time while I was maneuvering the plane, I just imagined Dave sitting next to me. I tried not looking over and seeing an empty seat.

I was sure I would panic, realizing I was all alone flying the Cessna 152. Concentrating on my right-hand turn, I must admit I was quite nervous, as it was critically important not to fly into any airspace that I had not been cleared for. Another small airport was close to us, and it had a different radio frequency, which meant no communication between us.

I had the runway in sight. I started to slowly pull back the throttle, which reduced the power, put down one flap at a time (which is the same as brakes in a car), and got ready for touch down as the runway came closer and closer. I could feel my hands holding on o the yoke so hard that my knuckles turned white. Then touch down followed, so smooth and perfect I could hardly believe it myself, considering it was my first solo landing. I must say it was a feeling that is difficult to describe; it must be felt. One successful solo takeoff and landing, two more to go!

After another thirty minutes of flying and two more touch and go's, I got out of the plane. Dave was waiting for me.

"Well? Did I pull it off okay?"

"Butter."

What on earth? Why did he say "butter"? What was he talking about?

"You didn't just pull it off, Victoria. It was like landing in butter. Amazing. I watched you from the ground. You are taking to this like a duck to water."

It was just great. I must say I was proud of myself. As a child, I often was told I would never amount to anything, but at this moment, I knew that they were all wrong.

As I continued to log more hours into my logbook, a new world opened up to me. I enjoyed landing a lot, sometimes so much it was flawless. Not bragging, but at times you couldn't even feel the plane touching the ground! Takeoff was good too. I loved the challenge that flying gave me. I needed it. It was an important step in freeing myself from my restricting early years.

A dozen or so flight hours later, I was ready to pilot my first night flight, with a licensed pilot at my side, of course. This would be a night to remember!

My dear friend Richard was not only a great physician but also an experienced, licensed pilot. He accompanied me on this round-trip flight to collect my daughter, Valentina, from college. At that time, she was a freshman in Upstate New York where she studied psychology.

We took off from the airport in Farmingdale to go pick her up. It was the fastest way to take her home to Long Island for the weekend, to avoid five-plus hours of car traffic.

Our plane was a Cessna 172 that belonged to a mutual friend. The flight was uneventful, which is a good thing of course. It was an afternoon in autumn. Looking out of the cockpit down under us, I saw all the wonderful different colors of the trees. How beautiful was Mother Nature!

Once we arrived and picked up Valentina, it didn't take long for us to prepare for our return to the Farmingdale airport. Everything we needed to pack up in the Cessna was done, and we were ready for our way back. The return flight was scheduled to take approximately two hours.

By that time, the autumn days were on the brink of twilight. As our plane took off up into the sky, the sun was just beginning its descent for what would soon become a spectacular sunset. As we witnessed its gradual drop on the horizon, the evening's darkness crept slowly, eventually surrounding our plane. In the distance, we could see lights sparkling. They were the lights of New York City approaching, closer and closer. Halfway through our flight, the picture of the grand city became more outlined, ever more vivid as if a real-life photograph was developing before our eyes. New York City looked like a silhouette, the outlines of the Twin Towers (this was ten years before 9/11) and Empire State Building tall and iconic in the background.

There was silence. In the plane, we all seemed paralyzed by the unspeakable beauty in front of us. All I heard was the soft murmur of the plane's engine. Every so often, I heard almost sacred whispers of "Beautiful" or "Unbelievable" or "Breathtaking." We were afraid to talk. It could ruin the moment.

I had been on numerous commercial flights in my life, many of them landing at night. But I never experienced a moment like this. Flying in a much smaller plane like a Cessna just gave me the feeling of being connected with the moment. A Cessna moves slower and also lower, of course, closer to the earth. This afforded us more time to bask in the glorious view. In a commercial airplane, all you have is that small window to look out. In a Cessna, you have windows all around, which makes you feel like you are right above all of that paradise-like beauty.

As I looked down, I saw the Hudson River right under us. It was sidling its way through the mountains like a snake, seducing the reflection of the lights of New York City. It was beguiling, a slithering, silvery snake of a river. Every so often, we saw the lights of other small planes. I wondered if the people in those planes were having the same emotions we were having. How could they not? How wonderful life can be!

The radio transmission of the big one, the JFK tower, interrupted my thoughts. "Identify yourself and give your exact location," the voice commanded. Communicating with the big one, the JFK tower, was another highlight of this night flight. It was the big time, so exciting! I'm sure I caught the attention of other pilots because it's not common to hear a woman's voice talking to JFK tower.

"November 186 Yankee requesting clearance to enter JFK airspace."

We had to wait for a few minutes to get an answer; after all, we were not the only one requesting to enter JFK airspace. It was a very busy time, and planes from different parts of the world were given priority to land. I had to slow down a bit, pulling back the throttle, a device controlling the flow of fuel or power to the engine to stay out of JFK airspace, as we were waiting for clearance. It was very interesting listening to all the different planes one by one requesting to land. Then finally it was our turn. We were given the okay to pass through JFK airspace. After getting clearings from the JFK tower, we continued to our destination of Farmingdale airport.

Then I got ready for our landing, lined up the glide path, and landed us safely. After our smooth "butter" landing, we busily unpacked everything for the ten-minute car ride home. Tired, I went to sleep. Even now, years later, I still think about this particular flight. It showed my competence with flying, making the trip myself to pick up Valentina. It showed me what I was capable of. And it was an awe-inspiring, stunning experience I will never forget.

Chapter 10

THE SEARCH FOR MY SISTER

I HAD PROMISED myself when I got back to the States after my brief moves back and forth, I was going to put some effort into finding my sister who had been adopted by an American military couple decades before. I wasn't exactly sure how to go about it, and this was pre-Internet. No way to use Google or Ancestry.com.

However, I knew the Red Cross was an organization that helped a lot of families find their loved ones and reunited them. I wrote them a letter explaining my desire to find my long-lost sister. I waited weeks and months but never received an answer. I was very frustrated; I was new to all this and did not know what else to do or where else to go.

In the spring of 1989, I had run to the supermarket. As I waited at the cash register, I took one of the magazines called *Woman's World* and started to look through the pages. I turned the first page and to my surprise saw a story I found extremely interesting. At the top of the page, the headline read, "Where are they now?"

It was an article focused on readers who sent in stories and pictures of someone they were looking for. *This may be my chance to find my sister*, I thought.

I bought the magazine to get more details. I was quite nervous. I found out how to reach the magazine and then had to look for a photo to send them. I not only had a family photo but also one of the couple who took my sister. I sent the photo and my story to the magazine.

A few months went by, and when I didn't hear anything, I kind of dismissed my mission. Then one day I received a letter from the magazine, telling me that they would print my story in the August 22, 1989, edition. I was anxious and could not wait, wondering if I'd have more luck this time finding my sister. And if so, what would she be like? Was she looking for me as much as I was looking for her?

So many questions went through my head. On August 22, I was the first one in line to pick up a copy of *Woman's World*, and then I rushed home to read my story. Not even thirty minutes later, I received several phone calls from people who said they knew my sister, now named Mildred, and that she was living in Arizona now and had two children, a boy and a girl.

I was all excited, feeling that I was getting close to my goal. One of the callers gave me a phone number to try. I thanked her and then hung up the phone, took a deep breath, and picked up the phone again.

To my surprise, someone who sounded like a teenage boy answered the phone.

"Can I speak to your mom?" I asked the boy.

"She's out but should be back shortly," he answered.

"Is it possible for her to call me when she gets home?"

"Yes, I will give her the message." I left my name and phone number and then hung up the phone.

Not even one hour later, my phone rang. "Hello, who is calling?" I asked. For a short moment, I heard nothing.

"It's me, Kristina," the woman on the other end replied.

"Sorry, you must have the wrong number," I said. "I'm looking for someone by the name of Mildred."

"Yes, this is me," she said. "My name used to be Mildred, but they changed it to Kristina."

It startled me a little, but I guess it made sense. Many children who were adopted were given new names by their new parents.

It took me a second to collect myself. "How much do you remember from before you got adopted?" I asked. I wanted to make sure I was talking to the right person.

"I remember a lot," Kristina said. "I knew I had sisters and brothers. I just don't know too many details anymore because I was so little when they took me."

"Kristina, I'm your sister! They took you from the orphanage, and I never knew what happened to you. You have no idea how long I was searching for you. Not a day went by without a thought of you, how you were doing and if you were happy."

"Yes, Vicky, I had similar thoughts." We both were silent for a bit. Then she went on, "I was adopted because my adopted mother thought she could not have any children. But about a year later, she got twin boys, and another year after the twins, she got another boy, plus the boy my adopted dad brought into the marriage. I was the only girl in the family."

We talked for a bit longer, and before we hung up the phone, I asked her to come and visit me in New York. Since I was working at a travel agency, I got a great deal on a plane ticket. About a month later, Kristina came to visit.

Her plane arrived at Long Island MacArthur Airport, a small airport only twenty minutes from my house. Valentina and I went to pick her up. We waited at the gate; everyone came out, then finally there was Kristina! It was a strange feeling. Although I knew she was my sister, not growing up together had made a huge difference; the familiar bond was not there.

Kristina stayed a whole week. We talked a lot. She brought photos from when she was a little girl, and looking at them, I knew she had to be my sister because I remembered most of the photographs. We had a wonderful week together before she returned to Arizona. I told her I would be visiting her next, to meet the rest of her family. Today, almost twenty-eight years later, we are still in touch, calling each other regularly.

Chapter 11

DETOUR WITH A YOUNGER MAN

"OH, FRANK," I beseeched. "I need a whole new room built on my house! Tell me you know someone for the job!"

Frank was a terrific bricklayer who was in the process of building me a brand-new driveway. "Sorry, Vicky, my specialty is bricks. I am not to familiar with doing construction on a house."

"I need to get this done; do you know anyone else?"

"Well, there is a young guy I can recommend. He worked on my crew a few times, and he's available.""

"He can't be as good as you!"

Frank smiled. "He does good work. I've heard

nothing but good about him. Everybody loves him. You should give it a try!"

Later the same day, Frank called "the young guy" to come over to my house.

"Glad to meet you, Andrew. How are you?"

Andrew was not what I expected. In fact, Andrew was far more than I pictured him to be. A native of Brazil, he had curly black hair, black piercing eyes, and skin the color of milk chocolate. And a fit, toned body that showed his build, one that you would expect to see in a calendar of the twelve most gorgeous carpenters of the year.

Frank had told me Andrew was young and fairly new at construction work. So of course I pictured the usual stereotype: a swaggering, brash, full-of-himself twenty something. But no. Andrew was on the quiet side, soft-spoken, well mannered, even subdued.

Over the next eight months, I hired him intermittently for various jobs and was pleased with his work. Always on time, thorough and courteous, Andrew had a sweet, appealing smile. There was a kind of shyness in his manner. If he was aware of how handsome he was, he certainly did not have a prom king attitude about it.

"That new boy working for you—what a hottie!" My neighbor Lilian was friendly, a little loud, and always outspoken. She didn't miss a trick. Her gaze pierced at me, and she gave me a big grin. "What's going on with that?"

"What do you mean?' I was innocent, quite oblivious to whatever she was trying to pry out of me.

"Listen, Victoria. When you get to be my age, you'll learn you have the right to say what's on your mind. No beating around the bush." Well into her seventies, Lillian was spry and healthy, as you'd expect a Pilates/yoga devotee to be.

"Okay, but I still don't know what you're asking me."

"Oh really? You mean you haven't noticed the way Hottie Boy is checking you out whenever you walk by or whenever you're around? He's always sneaking looks at you, but you haven't noticed? Hard for me to believe, dearie."

I was stunned. What? Andrew was at least twenty years my junior at the time. I hadn't noticed anything, so I responded as if I couldn't have cared less. For one thing, I didn't want Lillian gossiping around the neighborhood about an imagined affair with my youthful contractor.

"Your imagination is out of control, Lillian. Andrew's a nice, polite young man." Still, her surprising observation sparked something in me. Me? Enter into a romantic relationship with a younger man? And that odious word "cougar." Ugh! *Just what I need*, I pretested to myself. A young, good-looking guy hanging around to constantly remind me that I'm older than he is, that I'm the "older woman."

Was this some kind of reverse vanity? I think it was, on my part, because I was viewing the possibility of Andrew's attraction to me through the lens of my own personal vanity. Me—it was still all about me and my feelings. How would I react to other people's glances as they shook their heads with pity, no doubt? "Another middle-aged woman in denial about the fact she's not a kid anymore." "Cradle robber." And worst of all, "Cougar!"

No, I told myself, I was not about to slip into the role of the "older woman" anytime soon. I had already become too engrossed in this new era in my life, the inevitability of aging on the horizon.

But it was too late. Lillian's words took root, and I allowed myself to start paying attention to Andrew when he was around. I caught him looking at me, stealing glances with those hazel eyes that followed me. Could it be true? As weeks rolled along, he became gradually bolder yet always subtle and with a boyish charm.

"Hey, where've you been hiding?" I'd ask.

His face would light up instantly with what appeared to be genuine pleasure to see me. It was also too late for me to forbid his entrance into my thoughts. How many evenings I sat in my living room pondering his toned young body, his face and arms, strong and fine. No one, and I mean no one, knew how tempted I was to grab one of his stolen looks and take it further, to surrender to my increasingly visceral preoccupation with this man. At this stage in my life, I knew a few things abut men of any age. When a man shows interest in a woman, there is that element of anticipation, the testosterone-fueled hope that he will be intimate with her eventually. He hopes to experience her naked, along with the desire for pleasure. The irresistible mystery of the first seduction …

How long, I wondered, could I delay getting together with a man whose hormones were still in their raging prime? What was worse, his attraction to me was arousing my sexual desires as I surrendered to my own fantasies about us. Together, what would it be like? What kind of lover would he be? It was torture, yes. But harder and harder to endure. I had to put a stop to it.

I amazed myself as I discovered, for the first time, how in control I was! This was a new realization. I saw that my way of thinking had changed because I was going beyond my desires. I was beginning to consider the long-term consequences of my choices and actions. Now I was going a step further, from sexual reverie to thoughts about the inevitable mornings after, the eventual outcome. I forced myself to face it—a dead end. Cul-de-sac. There was nowhere for me to go with a man twenty-three years younger!

Someday he will surely want a family, which leaves what option for us? A sexual fling? I would have none of that. Mistakes I'd made when I was younger, often jumping on every impulse, had taught me well at last. (Look at the Dr. John situation and how that ended.) This was my triumph, the fact that my thinking had matured, revealing a wisdom I previously didn't own. I confess I did enjoy innocent flirting with him as time went on, smiles and joking banter.

About eight months into our first project, Andrew and I were discussing some more work that I needed him to do. Not concerned about usual conversation segues, he abruptly announced, "I had a dream about you, Vicky."

Uh-oh.

What happened in your dream? Words I couldn't say in return; words I didn't say. He was clearly expecting the question, but I did not ask. My solution was to ignore his in-my-face declaration. The look on his face was unforgettable. Tormented by his face wearing that fallen look, I punished myself with guilt for weeks afterward because I knew I hurt his feelings. What was he standing there feeling but a painful rejection?

Waiting for the right moment, I planned to tell him I didn't want to hurt him and I didn't want to be hurt either, that I couldn't waste his time—to gently explain there could be no intimacy between us. A romantic relationship between us had no future.

***

It was on a weekend, a nice fall day. I decided to take a walk to the beach of the Atlantic Ocean, which was only eight miles from my house. Summer season was gone, and the beach was almost empty with only a few sun worshipers. I was going to take advantage of the nice days we had left because winter was around the corner, and a walk on the beach would soon be out of the question.

I bundled up in warm clothes knowing that the Atlantic Ocean beach could be quite windy. I started to walk toward the beach, heading east. The waves were pretty high, and the wind blew around me as I was breathing in the fresh air. As I continued going east, I noticed less and less people. I picked a nice quiet place to sit down. I took off my shoes and socks and walked toward the ocean. It felt nice to feel the water and sand under my feet. It gave me great pleasure to watch the waves rolling up to the shore, endless and soothing. I sat down a few feet from the water, watching some brave surfers taking advantage of the huge waves. I envied their courage. It must take a lot of energy to ride such big waves.

I looked toward the west of the beach then

back to the east, which looked pretty empty by now, as most of the beach-goers were heading home. Far out in the distance, I saw the outline of a person, a silhouette against the setting of the sun. I couldn't make out if it was a man or a woman, as I faced the sun and it blinded me. Clearly, I wasn't the only one coming here to take advantage of that beautiful autumn day.

I continued watching the surfers, and every so often I looked over in the direction the person was coming from. As he came closer, I could see it was a man. I leaned back and kept looking at the few surfers enjoying riding the waves. I guessed it to be high tide, judging by the size of the waves. The beach became quieter around me. All I could hear every so often were the seagulls calling out at each other, accompanied by the roaring of the ocean, which was like a lullaby to my ears.

Deep in my thoughts, I felt someone tapping my shoulder. I turned around, and to my surprise, it was Andrew. "What are you doing here?" I asked.

"No special reason. I had some time on my hands and thought to take advantage of this beautiful day, taking a walk on the beach. It looks like we both had the same idea. Is it okay if I sit with you?"

"Sure. We can watch the sunset together."

Andrew made himself comfortable next to me. We both watched the bright red sun slowly disappearing into the ocean. As the sun went down behind the horizon, a little chill came over me.

Andrew noticed it and put his arm around me, like protection to keep me warm. "Lean against me. It will help you to stay warm."

I moved closer to Andrew, and as he held me tight, I was glad for his generosity and being so close to him. We sat there in silence watching the sun disappearing little by little, sharing a moment of serenity. To my surprise, Andrew's presence felt so comforting, a feeling so welcome to me. I couldn't remember the last time I felt like that. I stepped out of my comfort zone and put my head on his shoulder, enjoying the moment.

Andrew must have taken this gesture as a sign of acceptance for allowing such physical closeness. He then took my hand into his and held it on his chest. "Can you feel it, Vicky?"

"What are you talking about?" I was a little puzzled by his question.

"My heart, Vicky. It's my heart, beating for you."

"Yes," I softly whispered back. "Yes, Andrew, I can feel it."

"Do you feel what you are doing to me? Please tell me you are feeling the same!"

I leaned back and took a deep breath, looking toward the sunset. My silence must have been like torture for him.

He leaned over to me and softly whispered in my ear, "Let me be your man, Vicky, please. You have no idea the kind of torture it is for me to see you and not be able to be close to you."

I took a deep breath. "Andrew, it's not you." It was all I could say.

"Then what is it, Vicky?"

"I don't know. I just don't know."

"Okay then, but don't you think I deserve an answer?"

Yes, I knew that was the least I could do—give him an answer. But I couldn't. I just couldn't. With a silent gaze, I looked out to the open sea, hoping to find the right words. The main issue was the twenty-three years between us. We'd spoken about it many times, and many times he told me that this was not a problem for him, but unfortunately, it was a problem for me.

His desire to be close to me became stronger by the minute. Very gently, he kissed me on my forehead. I did not protest. I almost forgot what passion felt like. His kisses became more intense, and his passion was as hot as the sun in his native country of Brazil, so very powerful like the roar of the ocean!

I wasn't in control anymore, and I just didn't care. I not only allowed his advances; I welcomed them. His touch was wonderful. I closed my eyes and enjoyed every second of it. I wanted to hold on to the moment, not letting go. He continued kissing me slowly, down my neck, my breasts, my legs, toward my feet; no way was I going to stop him. At that moment, my intention of not being involved with him blew away in to the ocean breeze.

The cool water lapped at my feet, startling me. I opened my eyes, sat up, and looked around, but nobody was there. "Where did Andrew go?"

I must have fallen asleep; it was just a dream. Or not?

Chapter 12

FRIENDS, NOT LOVERS

"ALTHOUGH WE CAME from two different worlds …"

Two years later, about 1995, I was again facing my war against aging, every battle all on my own. Then an important insight hit me: my anxiety about aging had been suspended during my time with Werner. It was an oasis in the middle of my personal ocean of fear. It had ebbed and flowed with my flirtation with Andrew as well. Lonely and vulnerable, I now felt that I was going nowhere.

My bubbly friend Karen had a knack for good timing. She knew about Werner and my dramatic choice to not follow him back to Germany. Ever the cheerleader for love, this time her agenda was to convince me to meet a man she was acquainted with, a man who was twenty-three years my senior. In fact he was her lawyer.

"The thing is he's a widower and a workaholic. All he does is work. He's smart, well educated, of course, and very sophisticated. Been alone for years now, so now he's looking for someone. He just wants a friend, a female friend. A perfect gentleman! Are you interested?"

Seeing the expression on my face, my stern "You know how I feel about being fixed up" look, she countered with, "He is lonely, and he works all the time."

"Okay, why not," I said to Karen. "You can give him my phone number and have him call me."

Aaron turned out to be a blessing the moment he came into my life. It often felt like he was taking my hand into his, guiding me through the tough times. When he and I first met, I didn't know that an especially tough time would eventually be forthcoming in my future.

It was a Friday happy hour at a charming place called the Fighter Squad in Farmindale, New York. Near the airport where I took flying lessons, it was a cozy club made to look like a bunker, where you go when sirens are warning of an enemy attack. Some areas were like living rooms with a fireplace. A glass wall faced the runways so you could watch small aircraft taking off and landing.

I was on time, but Aaron was not. Twenty minutes later, he walked in. From the look of it, I could see he was an elegant man with a lot of class. We introduced ourselves, and he was apologetic right away. "I'm sorry to keep you waiting, Victoria. I had to finish up with a client."

My first impression of him was very positive. He had manners, style, and class. He sat down at our table and ordered a scotch and soda. We slipped easily into a pleasant conversation. We talked about me, him, and our interests. A connection sparked between us right away. On my end, it was admiration. He was mature, grounded, and good humored. Karen knew what she was talking about when she described him as a perfect gentleman.

Turns out we came from two different worlds. In fact, we were kind of opposites. There was the age difference, to begin with. Also, he was highly educated, having earned multiple advanced degrees. Conservative, laid back, and cautious, he was a serious thinker. A native New Yorker, Aaron was an urban-loving American sophisticate.

I, on the other hand, was lively, impulsive, and borderline high strung. My childhood in my native Germany was more rural and countrified. We balanced each other out well. Our first meeting turned out to be a wonderful evening. We made plans for a second dinner date. He took my phone number and wrote it on a napkin.

Many more dinner dates followed, and our friendship blossomed. Aaron introduced me to a world of new experiences. A bona fide Manhattanite, he escorted me to the finest restaurants in New York City, Broadway shows, and celebrity fundraisers. With him, I felt like a celebrity on the red carpet. Aaron gave me an anchor. His laid back personality anchored me. My predisposition to worrying and hyperactivity subsided in his presence. Serenity, a sense of calm, and a peaceful, safe feeling blessed me whenever I was with him. He was my rock.

I loved his approach, which was to simply take life as it comes, to enjoy things, including the little things. "Stop fretting, Victoria. Don't stress. To worry is useless because worry changes nothing. Don't freak out before you find a solution."

Aaron was a levelheaded, analytical,

logic-centric problem solver. For three years, we enjoyed each other's company and had lots of good times.

He was fond of telling me, "You make me feel young." Born to be a lawyer, he loved his work. A recurring pearl of wisdom from him was: "Don't shoot all your ammunition at once. Keep them wondering what's coming next." He was my one-man support group. Whenever I needed him, he was there. He gave me advice and taught me patience, something I still occasionally struggle with. Three years into our friendship, we knew each other well.

Of course Aaron knew all the best restaurants and clubs in Manhattan, and they knew him. He was welcomed and treated like royalty wherever we went. At the Four Seasons restaurant one evening, I was not my usual vivacious self. "What's bothering you?"

Startled at his question, I should have known better than to imagine I could conceal anything from him. "You're working too hard at being happy tonight. Why?"

"Am I that transparent? Aaron, I wanted to be brave!"

Troubled by that remark, he clearly expected an explanation from me. His face, without saying another word, was asking me for an explanation.

"There's been some bad news." My eyes focused on the tablecloth. I wasn't afraid! Yet my emotions were bullying me that night. They were controlling my behavior, and I didn't know why. I truly believed I wasn't afraid. "It seems I've been diagnosed with cervical cancer."

"But, dear, you're my best friend. You know I'll do anything I can to help you with this."

"Oh, Aaron, you are my best friend! You give me more than I ever hoped for! I wanted to show you how much stronger I am since I've known you. Honestly, I'm not afraid!"

The truth was I wasn't afraid of the cancer so much. It was the treatment regimen of radiation, the many doctors' visits for regular checkups on the blood count, and the thoughts of chemo that were exhausting. I'd hoped I could do without those, but it was not to be.

I was forty-four years old. My daughter was away at school, and I didn't have a huge support system in place.

Throughout the entire ordeal, he was the one

visiting me in the hospital, doing all the necessary things while I was disabled and weak from the surgery. At one point, I weighed eighty-five pounds. It was Aaron, my rock, who took care of everything. He ordered food to be delivered to my house so I didn't have to cook. Although he was in demand as a lawyer, he managed to find time to chauffeur me to and from doctors' appointments. With his tremendous support, I made an excellent recovery. Life went on.

As when I had been with Werner, my fear-of-aging disorder was completely suspended while I was with Aaron. You could say it was in remission. In any case, Aaron continued to be a treasured companion. Although I was forty-five and he was sixty-seven when we first met, I remember noticing from the beginning that age was not a factor and certainly not an issue for him. Seeing this man so comfortable with himself and his age, I was inspired, thinking of new ways of life, new ways of helping others.

"I was thinking, Aaron. I should become a psychiatrist."

"Do it!" He endorsed this notion with his usual can-do energy. He never whined or complained about getting older like some people do. With every breath he breathed, he inhabited an aura of positive energy. It was catching.

As the years went by, our friendship grew closer and closer. We had known each other for at least five good years, and an early "good morning" phone call from him became a daily routine.

On November 20, 2001, rushing to get ready for the day, I noticed the phone didn't ring as usual. Telling myself he probably got involved in a work-related matter, I dismissed it for a while. But as noon came around and still no call, I became a little worried. I tried his car phone, then his home phone, but there was no answer. His secretary was off that day, so I furiously called every number I had for him.

Time passed, and with no word from Aaron, I really started to worry. This was not like him. Then I called his daughter, who was also a lawyer in New York City. She told me that she had been trying to get a hold of him too. That capped it.

I dropped everything and drove over to his house. His dark blue Jaguar was parked in front, not a promising sight. More nervous by the minute, I knocked on the frond door repeatedly.

"Aaron! Are you there?" No answer. I had a key to his house.

My heart was pounding so badly it seemed it might come out of my chest. As I entered, I kept calling his name. "Aaron! It's me, Victoria. Where are you?"

Standing in the living room, I noticed the kitchen light was on. Then my eyes moved toward the bedroom. In sunny broad daylight, the bedroom ceiling light was on, signaling a foreboding scene. Instead of stepping faster, my feet slowed down. The bedroom door was open. It felt like it was threatening me. Each footstep was more painful than the previous one.

Pacing myself and drawing closer, I could see the lamp from the bed stand broken and crashed on the floor. Warily, I reached the bedroom. My heart froze. Aaron was sprawled face down on the floor, one leg twisted under the other. A hand was clinging to the phone, which had also crashed to the floor. I tried to shake Aaron and kept calling his name, my voice choking in my throat.

I called 911, struggling to speak clearly. Waiting for the ambulance, my mind was paralyzed. I was not able to think at all. Minutes later, the paramedics and police walked into the room. Aaron was pronounced dead on the spot. He had a massive heart attack.

It was too much for me. I had to get out of there. Given the okay to leave, I drove away from the house. *It's my fault!* Panic and sorrow gripped me. I could not shake the image of his fallen body with the phone in his hand. It told me he was trying to reach out for help! *It's my fault!*

Many times since then, I've blamed myself, over and over asking, why didn't I pay attention to the signs of this forthcoming tragedy? Weeks before his heart attack, he'd mentioned having very bad heartburn. He would be out of breath too easily, and I also noticed signs of his body looking bloated, holding water, a clear sign that his heart was not doing its job.

Not even a week later, Aaron was gone. It was like the foundation was ripped out from under me. My life came to a stop. There I was, at another turning point. What was I going to do now? I knew I would never again meet another person with such a good soul. I still think of him often and our precious time together. The hardest part of losing someone so close to your heart isn't so much having to say good-bye but rather learning to live without them. His fast passing didn't give me a chance to say good-bye. What would I have said?

In the end, he gave me a life perspective. It was built on the strength that can only come from the simple wisdom of genuinely liking yourself. It would take years for me to fully avail myself of his rich legacy. There is a song from Bette Midler, "Wind beneath My Wings." For me, he was all this if not more. I will cherish the time we had together for the rest of my life.

It must have been cold there in my shadow,
To never have sunlight on your face.
You were content to let me shine, that's your way.
You always walked a step behind.
So I was the one with all the glory,
While you were the one with all the strength.
A beautiful face without a name for so long.
A beautiful smile to hide the pain.
Did you ever know that you're my hero,
And everything I would like to be?
I can fly higher than an eagle,
For you are the wind beneath my wings.
It might have appeared to go unnoticed,
But I've got it all here in my heart.
I want you to know I know the truth, of course
I know it.
I would be nothing without you.
Did you ever know that you're my hero?
You're everything I wish I could be.

Chapter 13

DON'T BE BITTER, BE BETTER

I'VE OFTEN ASKED myself, "Why did I have such a strong urge to return to this place?" Once a year whenever time permitted, I like to fly home to the country where I was born, Germany. Often I would take my daughter and her two boys with me because I wanted them to be acquainted with their heritage.

During all of those previous visits with my family, I had relived memories of my early childhood. Growing up in an orphanage was no fun. Especially in post–World War II Germany. It was, as I've described before, literally a prison for children. The only bright spot we experienced was that once a year the children between ages ten and thirteen were taken on a one-week vacation to the Atlantic Ocean or Austria. These once-a-year visits were the only fond memories I had of growing up as an orphan.

Situated directly to the south and slightly east of Germany, Austria captivated me. This spectacularly beautiful place with enormous mountains left a powerful impression on me as a child. They were huge, towering over us, feeling so high that it looked like they were reaching the sky. The opening of this land gave me a sense of being free, no walls or restrictions; here I could breathe! For me, Austria was a place of calmness and serenity in the middle of a grim life.

Fast-forward to one day in the midst of my battle against aging, around 2008. I decided to return to Austria, the wonderful place I had such strong feelings for. But this time I knew I had to do this trip alone. It was a time when I felt the lowest in my life, going through a period of forced acceptance that my youth was behind me, over. I just had to go back to Austria. I felt like there was something else I left behind, something I had to recapture one more time to close this chapter. It was something more than the desire to reclaim good childhood memories that were so scarce.

And still, I asked myself, why do I need so badly to return?

I prepared for this, my first solo visit to Austria. There was no relationship in my life at this time; Werner, John, and Aaron were now in the past. Nothing was stopping me from doing what I wanted to do, which was to move on, find out which direction I was going in. I was fifty-nine, and it seemed age was creeping up faster and faster, and as long as I was capable of doing what I felt like doing and as long as I was able to, I was not going to let anything stop me.

As my departure date approached, I was one bundle of nervous energy. In no time, I found myself sitting in a plane at JFK, preparing to head east toward Germany, not looking forward to the seven-hour flight. That part I could do without. After takeoff, our evening meal was served. Soon after came the movie and then relaxing and trying to get some sleep. But I could not get comfortable. Too many thoughts were rushing through my head.

Again I asked myself, "Why do I have such a strong urge to return to this place?"

I stirred some hours later when the pilot's voice

over the speaker system roused me. "We will be reaching our destination shortly."

Apparently I had dozed off for two or three hours. Flight attendants began serving breakfast, and soon after that we were told to get ready for a landing at the Frankfurt, Germany, airport. All passengers were rapt, our gazes focused on the runway as we got closer. Touch down! We were there!

Everyone busily gathered their belongings to deplane, including me. Suitcase in hand, I made my way through customs and immigration, then over to collect my rental car. Off I went on another long journey, a five-hour drive to the apartment in Austria that I had rented for this solo visit.

Upon arrival, I was pleased to see a small but charming mini-cottage waiting for me. My little cottage was surrounded by beautiful mountains, pure nature, and fresh air. The only sounds I heard were the birds singing and a small river nearby running down from the mountain. The mountain water was so clean I could see all the way to the bottom of it. It was water from snow melting on top of the mountain.

I was fatigue from not sleeping enough on the

plane, and adjusting to the six-hour time change was taking its toll. But there was no way I was ready to lie down and get some rest. I was way too wound up!

What was I anticipating? I went to the window and opened it to welcome some fresh mountain air into my diminutive temporary abode. All my eyes could see for miles around were snow-covered mountains. How much more beautiful could it get? Like an old-fashioned picture postcard but it was up close and real!

Seeing this vision of nature is something I honestly cannot describe. I felt as though the environment tingled every one of my human senses. The air was crisp and cool; the colors were rich and vibrant, and even the sounds of bells on the goats felt magical and charming to me. One thing I missed so much was the food, which is out of this world. So I ventured out for a bite to eat. After a great meal, I returned to my cottage, hoping at least to rest, and rest I did. I awoke the next morning from an excellent night's sleep and decided to be a tourist. Sightseeing is what it was all about after all.

I would see all the familiar places, including

the salt mines, the famous lake called Koenigsee, and of course the well-known mountain called Watzmann. I was flooded with memories of visiting all these places as a child. I couldn't get enough! I was absorbing everything like a sponge.

First I was going to take a tour to the old salt mine, the place where salt is literally taken from the earth. Salt mine tours were always included when we made these trips as children from the orphanage. Salt mines are all over Austria, and to visit one, there are no words to describe it.

When we arrived at the mountain, everyone was given a black jumpsuit to wear over our clothing, which made all of us look like salt miners. We were ordered to sit on wagons similar to wagons on a train. "Only six people to a wagon please. If one is full, take the next one!" shouted a voice over the loud speaker. "You will be driving down into the mountains, and at the end of the ride, you get off the train. You will meet your tour guide, who will then continue the tour with you. Please do not reach out. Keep your arms close to you. The tunnel is very tight. You can get hurt. The tour will take about one hour. Then we will meet you back up here."

We all got comfortable in our seats and held on tight to the metal bar in front of us. We started to roll, faster and faster, several hundred feet into the mountain. This is not an experience for anyone who is claustrophobic! At the end of the ride, our tour guide was waiting. When everyone was accounted for, we continued our tour. "Please stay close to each other and follow me. Do not wander off on your own because the mine has many tunnels where you can easily get separated from the group and get lost."

This sounded pretty scary. I was not about to get lost. It was a very dark place with only a few lights. I made sure I stayed close to our tour guide. After a few meters, the guide turned to us. "All of you form a line. Then four people at a time step forward to the slide, sit on it one after the other, and hold on to each other. When you arrive at the end of the slide, get off immediately so I can send the next set of four." It looked like a slide similar to one on a playground, only much longer. I must admit it was kind of fun as we zoomed a few hundred more feet into the mountain.

The rest of the tour was a walk down memory lane for me, literally. Once that far, there were many things, both interesting and educational. Our tour guide pointed out the huge salt mountains where salt was taken from, and then we crossed a small lake with a boat to get to the other side of the lake. This lake formed itself from the salt mountain, which changed into a condensed liquid due to the constant humidity so many kilometers under the earth.

We were told that this lake was so full of salt that anybody who falls into the lake will not go under, even if he does not know how to swim, because of its great salt content, which is similar to the Dead Sea in Israel, where the salt content is very high as well. It's also a big tourist attraction. In addition, this kind of salt in the water had a healing effect for the skin if you had a skin condition. After approximately one hour, the tour ended, and we were back up again. We then had to return our jumpsuits. It was a great day, we all agreed. Then we headed home.

The next day, I decided to visit the Koenigsee, a huge lake in Austria, another very famous tourist attraction. A boat would take us to the other side of the lake, which took about one hour, just to give you an idea of how big this lake really was.

As the boat slowly made its way to its destination, we passed great mountains as well as the famous Watzmann Mountain. All year, the tip of this mountain is covered with snow, looking like an ice-cream cone with a vanilla ice-cream topping.

At one point, the boat came to a stop, and the tour guide then took out a trumpet and played a few notes, which hollowed into the mountains and bounced off each of the seven mountains like an echo. It was truly music to my ears, the notes reverberating among those stunning mountains.

My stay in Austria was ten days. Each day I visited another tourist attraction, and before I knew it, it was nearly time to return to the United States. It was a clear day, one day before my departure, and I was eager to take advantage of it. A walk right into the mountains would be my final adventure. This was one thing I could never have done by myself as a child from an orphanage. We all had to stay in a group; nothing could be done individually. But now there was no one to tell me what I could or could not do; this feeling of freedom was new to me.

Right after breakfast, I prepared for a deliberately long walk. By that time, a cloud or two had drifted into the sky, but I refused to let that stop me. I began walking toward the snow-capped mountains. The higher I walked, a calmness sidled up to me, softly, like a secret. It was a welcome feeling and continued to grow with each step. Very high up, I heard everyday sounds in the distance below, a dog barking, sounds of a car engine …

Everything looked so peaceful. I noticed the same river from near my cottage, not very far from me, running down the mountain. I worked up a small sweat, which made me thirsty, and I needed a few sips of water to quench my thirst. I had no cup, so I used my hands. The water was ice cold but so refreshing and clean. It felt like heaven up there. Breathing in that fresh mountain air was heaven for my lungs, and all I could hear at that height were the birds and bells on the necks of the cows nearby. The cows and the farmers stay up there in the mountains all summer long. Butter and cheese are made from the milk and once a week are picked up by someone from the village to be sold. The cows are taken back down in autumn. The farmers then decorate the cows with flowers as a sign that all went well, no cows got sick or fell off a cliff (which happened on occasion), and bring them down back to the village. For the farmers and the people/tourists, it is a huge event.

I must have walked at least one or two hours when I saw a bench right ahead of me. Perfect timing! I was ready to have a seat and absorb the illustrious scene I was now part of! From up so high, it was all so exquisite! Surrounded by illustrious mountains, I became aware of the fascination of nature quickly; it was this blend of boundless freedom. The view of the sky and the landscape that lay at my feet were pure romance with nature.

I gazed around contentedly and spotted the village where I was staying.

Everything looked so peaceful. Never before in my life had I perceived and experienced the beauty of nature until that moment. There is immeasurable beauty in a mountain view. It was such a peaceful place. It felt so comforting, like a security blanket. I felt so disconnected from the pressure of life; it was a welcome feeling. "Why did I feel so strongly about returning to this place?"

As I sat there calmly, I struggled to collect my thoughts; many things were running through my head. I sat there in silence for I don't know how long. I went backward in time, the time I visited this place as a child. I had no worries then and felt so free, as free as a child can feel, without all the pressure we face as an adult, and so unaware what life would bring …

Then I realized I was not that child anymore. I was going into my sixties. Sure I did not feel like it, but so many things reminded me how fast the years went by. To be an aging woman in a society where looks and beauty are so important was not an easy task, and as women, often we feel like damaged goods only to be put aside. The frustration and uncertainty of not being what I used to be was not easy to swallow. Losing that attractiveness I took for granted all my life was not easy to accept.

I was getting older, but what could I do about it? I was not the only one. The more I tried to hold on to the past, the faster time seemed to go by. I had a choice—either keep trying in vain to hold on to my youth and continue to be frustrated and unhappy—or let go and make the best out of it.

All of us have our own fears, and we are often near despair. Fear, worry, and anxiety will only paralyze your soul and will not let you go forward. We are not alone; however, we are the ones who have the power to choose.

I chose to let go. A quote went through my head, one from Louis Armstrong. "Thou shall not become bogged down by frustration, for 90 percent of it is rooted in self-pity and it will only interfere with positive action."

So true, I realized that day.

In those quiet moments, staring at those beautiful mountains, I realized there will always will be challenges in my life. I just had to find the courage to deal with them. I wanted to look at what I have rather than what I don't have. I had to let go of the past! I had to make the best out of it. A good cry is just as well as a good laugh. I did enough of this; it was time to look forward and not back anymore. There will always be a hello and good-bye whether we meet people or see them leave. It's part of life. It was time to say good-bye to negative thoughts and feelings, which were like heavy weights on my shoulders and only slowed me down.

I'll play my part in this spectacle called life and will do my best to flow with it, adjust and accept it totally, and as a result, I am sure I will find some peace within for myself and experience tranquility and satisfaction with what is.

In the far distance, I heard the sound of thunder, which seemed to echo off each mountain. I knew from the locals that in the mountains a thunderstorm could come up fast without warning, so I decided to walk back to the house. The years had widened the view, and that moment in the mountains made me realize I needed to let go of the struggle I had been fighting for some time.

Yes, I get older with each birthday, but I still have the mental energy of a young person. To worry too much can be draining, and you can lose a certain zest for life as well. I did not want to get bitter, I wanted to get better, a more positive outlook on my new life.

With a new view and new goals, there was no more feeling sorry for myself. Life has to go on. After all, I am not the only one going through these changes. I will accept it as it comes along.

I returned home to the United States. I picked

up where I left off, with the good intentions I had so many months before—to keep busy and concentrate on positive things. With age, my priorities have changed as well. I have learned to let go of things that became idols in my life. There is no room anymore for thoughts of things I cannot change, and I've started to embrace a more balanced lifestyle. I am sure every so often there will be a moment in my life when I feel invisible. Then I will look in the mirror and tell myself, "This is me now," and make the best of it.

"Beautiful young people are acts of nature, but beautiful old people are works of art."

Chapter 14

A FATEFUL CALL

In the summer of 2016 at six o'clock one morning, I heard the phone ring. I was asleep, and thinking it was a dream, I didn't react to it first. As the phone kept ringing, I realized it was not a dream.

Who would call me at this hour? I normally never picked up a phone that early in the morning, but for some reason, I decided to answer. A few days prior, I had sent my grandson to visit Germany for two whole months. I wanted him to get closer to the country of his ancestors and have more control of the German language. He had been there on a regular basis since he was three months old, and though he spoke some German, I felt it needed some brushing up.

I knew the call could not have come from

the United States. The only logical source would be Europe, since they were six hours ahead. I started to get a little nervous and was almost afraid to answer the phone, thinking the worst. I was hoping it would stop. I guess it was wishful thinking. I finally got up to answer the phone.

With a very nervous hello, I waited to hear who was on the other end. It seemed forever until I heard a woman's voice.

"Victoria, is this you?"

"Yes it is," I answered with a whisper.

"It's me, Lori," she said.

A big surge of relief came over me. Lori was a very good friend of mine for many years. She had emigrated with her family from Austria to South Africa (Johannesburg) some thirty years ago and now had a very successful business. Over the many years, we stayed in touch with each other by phone calls or e-mails. She kept asking me to visit them in South Africa, eager to show me the beauty of this country and take me to places unknown to tourists. Every single time, I accepted it but told them, "Not now but maybe next year." The years went by, however, and sadly I never got around to it, even though many times

I said to myself, "If not this year, maybe next year." I cherished the idea of having my personal tour guide showing me the country not too many tourists had seen.

My friend spoke shakily. "My Andy is gone!"

I did not understood right away. "What do you mean?"

"He died," she said. "Two weeks ago."

"Oh my God!" I felt paralyzed with shock. "What happened?" I asked.

"He had incurable cancer."

At this moment, I felt like reaching through the phone and holding her and letting her know I would be there for her and help her through her difficult time. I told her how bad I felt and to please call me anytime she had the need to talk to someone. "I will be there for you." Then we ended our conversation.

As I lay there in bed, my thoughts jumbled, I remembered how I enjoyed our friendship, both of them. Lori and Andy were the total opposite of me, so calm and collected. At this moment, Aaron came to mind and made me realize how fast life could be over. Andy had only been a few years my senior.

Why oh why did I keep putting off their invitation to the next year and the next year? I felt crushed. The news of his death felt so overpowering.

I thought I lived my life to the fullest, but now I knew that was not the case. Why else would I feel so remorseful about not taking the opportunity to visit them? Not only did I not get to see this beautiful country, but I also missed the opportunity to see my dear friends again.

I told myself this had to change! At one point, I wanted to be able to say, "This was my life!" and not question myself by asking, "Was this my life?"

Chapter 15

A FINAL WORD TO READERS

THE LAST TIME I was at Home Depot, I didn't really notice whether men were looking at me. I was involved in a project, and I just needed to get in the store and get the light-bulbs I needed. Visiting Home Depot was a reminder of the incident many years ago. It was the beginning of a struggle I was not prepared to accept at the time. Today I am more balanced and less vulnerable to negativity like the Home Depot incident. I am my own cheerleader in every way. I feel confident enough without the approval of a man. The wrenching effect from being invisible that I felt all those years ago is long gone.

I hope as you were reading this book you found some comfort in it. Foremost, I wanted you to know you are not alone. As we feel time and again how oppressive it can be, being aging women in today's society and going through different stages in our lives is not an easy task. I must admit I too had to learn to accept the changes—not only getting older in numbers but the physical changes as well. Looking good and feeling good is something to work on; it's not coming automatically anymore.

Plus, does any woman, no matter what age, ever want to lose that certain sex appeal? With the pressure from media and our culture, we may sometimes wonder, *What good would it do?* And then we end up not putting time and energy into ourselves.

In fact, for many men, their initial attraction to a woman is focused on a woman's looks. And I would be lying if I said that I'm 100 percent okay with being invisible in life and what comes with it. There are still moments I feel I am at my weakest, but today I accept the challenges about aging at a more settled pace. For me, the work and effort is toward being positive about the changes, reclaiming my power as an aging woman in this society, and focusing on moving forward.

So consider this: If you don't accept your natural aging process, then you're sending out negative waves, negative energy about yourself. As you look at yourself, you'll come to realize how things changed for you over the years. That should not mean that life has stopped. Perhaps you don't see yourself as appealing to your husband or partner anymore, if you have one. Have you ever thought about what could be the reason? Is it because your or his feelings have changed? How confusing it can be to think otherwise. Having the feeling of losing that spark can be devastating.

But life does not have to be like this. Changes are natural. You are the only one in control of it. Do not use this as an excuse and a reason to think otherwise. For example, we may tend to wear clothing for more practical rather than stylish reasons, which in turn has a huge impact on our physical relationships with our partners. If you want your relationship with your husband or partner to remain strong, look at yourself and ask yourself what changes you can make to improve the relationship.

Make a commitment to yourself to get back your self-esteem and ask yourself, "What can I do to make it better?" Stop putting them off with your lack of style. Start by wearing clothing that is more stylish than practical, and put on a little makeup! In doing this, not only will you look and feel fantastic, but it's sending out a positive message, and you will notice a positive change in him as well, certainly a most rewarding feeling.

To keep a relationship strong, it's worth the extra mile, and you will see a huge difference. Have you ever thought of giving your partner that special attention? If he comes home at night, take time to listen to him and what he has to say. Make him feel important. I personally believe in showing kindness when I talk to him. A little touch on his hand or cheek does wonders, a sign to let him know that he is just as important to me as I am to him. No, we don't need to meet him at the door all dressed up every time he comes home. There are so many other ways to keep that flame going. Have your imagination do the walking!

Make a commitment to yourself to branch out, to try something new that's a little out of your comfort zone. For me, it was learning to fly. That might not resonate with you, but how about learning to line dance? Or taking a pottery class?

Maybe you've always dreamed of doing something with your photography. Start a website with it! Sell some pictures on a stock photo site. Tag along and be an assistant for a wedding photographer. The point is to try something new, something that's about your dreams and aspirations. This will keep the focus off other people's opinions and more on your opinion about yourself.

Another area to focus on is your mind instead of your body. Of course, take care of your health; take care of your nutritional needs and the like, and consider doing something to improve your mind. Take a class in Eastern philosophy. Learn to cook real Italian with an Italian chef. Try your hand at doing a mosaic patio table. Stretching your mental capacity will have health benefits and help your mood. Trying—and succeeding— with a new skill will make you feel better about yourself and your life.

However, you do not always have to be in a relationship to have those positive feelings. To improve points in my life, I am not just doing it for a partner; now I am also doing it for myself. I once had a friend who put on makeup every day. She had no partner at the time.

"Why are you putting on makeup?" I asked her. "We are not going anywhere."

"Why not?" she answered. "I am doing it for myself. It makes me feel good." An answer I will always remember.

How right she was! From that day on, I started to put more effort in myself and do positive things. It most certainly lifts my spirit. If you want to overcome obstacles in your life, learn how to make a choice. Have yourself be guided by your ideas. You are the only one with control over yourself. Nothing is impossible if you set your mind to it. Always have a goal; it will motivate you to go on. I love languages, so I decided to learn my third language. I am sure each one of you will find something you enjoy. Then go after it without reluctance. This is the only life you have now—use it!

Getting used to a new stage in my life will take some adjustment, just like anything else. I have reached that moment, and I am okay with it. I don't feel threatened by the future anymore and take life one day at a time. I've hung up my gloves, and I no longer fight the aging process.

I hope my story has helped you in your journey

through aging and life. Stay positive, stay active, and stay engaged!

In my house, I have a framed poem hanging on my bedroom wall. You might find it inspiring too. Every so often, I read the words, which are very soothing for me.

Desiderata

Go placidly amid the noise and haste, and remember what peace there will be in silence. As far as possible without surrender be on good terms with all persons. Speak your truth quietly and clearly; and listen to others, even the dull and ignorant; they too have their story. Avoid loud and aggressive persons, they are vexations to the spirit.

If you compare yourself with others, you may become vain and bitter; for always there will be greater and lesser persons than yourself. Enjoy your achievements as well as your plans. Keep interested in your own career, however humble; it is a real possession in the changing fortunes of time. Exercise caution in your business affairs; for the world is full of trickery. But let this not blind you to what virtue there is; many persons strive for high ideals; and everywhere life is full of heroism.

Be yourself. Especially, do not feign affection. Neither be critical about love; for in the face of all aridity and disenchantment it is as perennial as the grass.

Take kindly the counsel of the years, gracefully surrendering the things of youth. Nurture strength of spirit to shield you in sudden misfortune. But do not distress yourself with imaginings. Many fears are born of fatigue and loneliness. Beyond a wholesome discipline, be gentle with yourself …

Printed in the United States
By Bookmasters